Get

- ❁ **WHO** made Brandy so nervous in the studio, she couldn't sing

- ❁ **WHAT** her favorite movies, meals, and clothes are

- ❁ **WHEN** she started her hugely successful acting and singing careers

- ❁ **WHERE** Brandy gets her song ideas

- ❁ **HOW** she feels about love, relationships, and stardom

- ❁ And much, much more!

Brandy
SITTIN' ON TOP OF THE WORLD

ANNA LOUISE GOLDEN
AN UNAUTHORIZED BIOGRAPHY

St. Martin's Paperbacks

NOTE: If you purchased this book without a cover you should be aware that this book is stolen property. It was reported as "unsold and destroyed" to the publisher, and neither the author nor the publisher has received any payment for this "stripped book."

BRANDY

Copyright © 1998 by Anna Louise Golden.
Cover photograph by Larry Ford/Outline.

All rights reserved. No part of this book may be used or reproduced in any manner whatsoever without written permission except in the case of brief quotations embodied in critical articles or reviews. For information address St. Martin's Press, 175 Fifth Avenue, New York, N.Y. 10010.

ISBN: 0-312-97055-2

Printed in the United States of America

St. Martin's Paperbacks edition / January 1999

10 9 8 7 6 5 4 3 2 1

FOR NOVA,

   Welcome to the World

ACKNOWLEDGMENTS

I always begin this way, but it's always true, so I'd like to say a big thank you to my agent, Madeleine Morel, without whom none of this would be happening for me. Glenda Howard, the editor of this book, is also wonderful, a person who goes for what she believes and makes it happen. I'm very grateful she made this happen.

Some of the research was done by Stacy Peloquin, who was not only spectacular in her thoroughness, but also *fast*. Thank you. Friends encouraged along the way, sometimes verbally cracking the whip, which might have been a good thing. So thank you to all of you—you know who you are. And, on the without-whom tip, thanks to my parents, without whom it would be someone else writing this book. Not only did they give birth, they also constantly gave me encouragement, and I've never forgotten it. L & G are both treasured and loved, as are Tasha, Zuni, Mardi, Boodle, Bina, and Sylvi. Snowy will never be forgotten.

The writing of this book was helped by the following articles: "Brandy," by Lynn Norment, *Ebony*, August 1998; "Cinderella Has Left the Building," by O.J. Lima,

Seventeen, September 1998; "Brandy," by Jocelyn T. Amador, *Black Hair Styles and Care Guide*, August 1998; "Upswing," by Jeremy Helligar and Amy Laughinghouse, *People*, August 3, 1998; *Word Up!: The Best of Rap and R&B Featuring Brandy and Monica*; "The Boy Is Mine," *Word Up!*, September 1998; *Right On!*, October 1998; "Starry-Eyed," by Ulrica Wihlborg, *People*, June 8, 1998; TV Fame Spurs Norwood, by J.R. Reynolds, *Billboard,* August 27, 1994; "When Down Is Up," *People*, November 21, 1994; "TV's *Moesha* Gives Positive View of Black Family," *Jet*, November 26, 1996; Teen Angel, by Betsy Sharkey, *Mediaweek*, February 19, 1996; "Brandy: Keeping It Real," by Rick Marin and Allison Samuels, *Newsweek,* March 25, 1996; "Brandy's Big Moment," by Janet Weeks, *TV Guide*, July 18-24, 1998.

INTRODUCTION

"I love to work. I want a star on Hollywood Boulevard. I want all of it. I want to win a Grammy."

Lots of people want those things. They dream of having it all, of being a big, famous star. But making those dreams come true is a different matter altogether. Brandy, who spoke those words, *is* going to have it all. There aren't too many girls that fly around, who have a show like *Moesha*, the most happening thing on the upstart UPN network. Or two multi-platinum albums, a handful of massive hit singles, including one that dominated the summer of 1998, and now her first movie, the guaranteed hit, *I Still Know What You Did Last Summer*, which pairs her with one of the other hottest babes on television, Jennifer Love Hewitt.

She's got it going on, all right. And it's only five years ago that she first appeared on television, playing Denesha on the ABC sitcom, *Thea*. You talk about coming a long way. . . .

Then again, it's a long way from Mississippi, where Brandy Norwood—which is her full name—was born, to Los Angeles. And the fact that she got there at all is due to the faith of her parents, Willie and Sonja Norwood, who believed so much in their daughter's potential that they made the trek across the country when she was four years old.

And faith does pay off. Brandy is probably the biggest African-American star to come into people's homes every week. Her show does well, not just for UPN, but up against all the other prime-time offerings.

Moesha may be a little sassy, very definitely cool, but Brandy herself is just Brandy. She's the girl who dated Wayna Morris of Boyz II Men for a year and a half, who went to the prom with future LA Lakers basketball star Kobe Bryant. And she's got the coolest hair on the tube.

Above all, she's a genuine, nice person. If her image comes across a squeaky-clean—no cussing, no fighting, no sex or drugs—it's because that's exactly the way Brandy is. It's not all hype; it's her, with no front, no pose. Others may try to come across that way, but for Brandy that's life.

She lives with her mom and dad and her little brother, Ray J. (whose real name is Willie Norwood, Jr. After acting on *The Sinbad Show*, he's now following in his sister's footsteps as a singer, with his own album out on Atlantic Records). She might be nineteen, but she's in no hurry to move out on her own. Everything is cool, so why change it?

Brandy can be generous to a fault. She has two cars, a Lexus GS-400 and a Range Rover. When Ray J. wanted to borrow the Lexus, she gave it to him.

Of course she can get moody, but who doesn't. Her idea of bitchiness, however, is a little different from most other people. For her, being bad is when "I'll get in my car and just drive and don't tell anyone where I am."

Of course, these days Brandy is in such demand that everyone needs to know where she is, twenty-four hours a day. Her mom and dad look after her career, and always have. Her mother, in fact, is quite the businesswoman, also handling the affairs of Ray J. (of course) and Mase.

It's not easy having your mom in your business *and* in your life every day, but it works, even though Brandy admitted that "We disagree all the time. My mom, we're best friends, but we fight like cats and dogs. We love each other to death, but we're so much alike . . . She's a good woman and I love her. And I want to be exactly like her."

Still, she can always turn to her father, and she does. "He lets me get away with things . . . He's so sweet. I don't understand how he can be just so sweet all the time, like nothing ever bothers him. He's like that *all the time*."

The business works because the family works together and always has. They've made Brandy into a megastar. There aren't many double threats around, but she's definitely one, who manages dual careers as both a singer and actress. Her self-titled debut album in 1994 brought her a huge hit single with "I Wanna Be Down," sold over four million copies, and gave her two Grammy nominations, for Best New Artist and Best Female R&B Performance (for "Baby"). Not a bad way to start out.

And by that time she was also a regular on *Thea,* amazing audiences every week. Then came *Moesha* in 1995, and Brandy came into her own as the coolest teen on television, no contest, no matter what color. She was a regular kid, with regular problems, living with a regular family. It was *real*, even if it wasn't quite Brandy's real life. Unlike her character, Brandy doesn't have a tattoo, nor would she ever think of getting one. Nor would she think of storming out of the house, vowing never to return, the way Moesha did at the end of the show's third season. But it worked. People believed her.

They also believed her when she played Cinderella in the 1997 ABC-TV special, stealing the show from a pair of major talents, Whoopi Goldberg and Whitney Houston—no mean feat for a teenager. But she's got the talent to do exactly that.

Her single, "Sittin' Up in My Room," which had appeared on the *Waiting to Exhale* soundtrack, also took the charts by storm in 1996 (as did other songs from the film). It alone sold over one million copies. Brandy was in the house, no two ways about it.

She finally released her second album in 1998, with a much more grown up Brandy on the cover of *Never Say Never*. The kid with her hair in bunches was history. Instead this was a lovely young woman (no wonder she'd signed a contract with Cover Girl and done some modeling) with long, gorgeous braids, and a whole different 'tude. The one thing that hadn't gone away was the voice. Instead, it had flowered into an incredibly mature instrument. She'd made the transition from teen to mature in one fell swoop. And the fact that it contained *the* song of the year, "The Boy Is Mine," her duet with Monica (with whom she's friends—there is no rivalry between them), didn't hurt anything. Everywhere you went during the summer, it was impossible to avoid that song. MTV, radio . . . there was simply no getting away from it, which pushed *Never Say Never* up the album charts, all the way to Number Two, going platinum (over one million copies sold) less than two months after it appeared in the stores. Meanwhile, "The Boy Is Mine" took the teen duet all the way to Number One, where it seemed to want to take up permanent residence in the top spot.

You could say that Brandy had arrived big-time. All the more so because she'd co-written six of the record's sixteen tracks, as well as recording a duet with Mase, her mother's other client, who also seemed to be all over the charts during the summer, alone, with other people, and with the ubiquitous Puff Daddy.

It was about as perfect a lead-in as she could have hoped for, with her first feature film coming out in the fall. *I Still Know What You Did Last Summer* was the sequel to the incredibly successful *I Know What You Did Last Summer*, which had helped propel Jennifer Love Hewitt into the really big leagues, taking in some $72 million at the box office. Now Brandy was to be cast as the college roommate of Love's character, Julie James, and the pair would embark on some rather gruesome adventures in the Bahamas.

The filming was actually done in April and May, in the small town of Tenacatita, and the shoot took Brandy away from home for the first time in her life, a kind of freedom she'd never known before, although the working hours were long and grueling. Not that she got wild, it's just not in her blood. The craziest thing she did was keep up with her family and friends on the phone, running up an $8,000 bill while she was out of the country, although she could certainly afford to pay it.

This is undoubtedly just the beginning of a movie career for Brandy, a chance to prove herself on the big screen, which has never been easy for people of color. But she comes in as an established star in her own right, the kind of person who'll draw people into the theaters just to see her, as well as the movie. Her *Cinderella* on television was a revelation. There'll be plenty more to come, parts that will give her the opportunity to both act and sing.

And then, of course, there's *Moesha*. That's not leaving the screen anytime soon. It's a chance for Brandy to grow up, albeit in public, and it's made her into a role model of sorts for teens. The set may not always be the friendliest place—she and Countess Vaughn, her co-star aren't exactly the best of friends, although they're "cool" when they work together—but the show jams.

Brandy has been lucky, and she knows it. She was born with her gift. But she's worked hard to make the most of it, and the place she now occupies. She learned a long time ago that things don't just happen; you have to *make* them happen.

But now, fully established, one of the big young stars of R&B (one with a major, major crush on Puff Daddy), of television, and soon to be of movies, too, she can look ahead. At nineteen, she's going to on the scene for a long, long time yet, and she has no plans to drop singing to concentrate on acting or the other way around. It may be exhausting, but she's learned that you really can do it all. She can get the Grammy, she can get that star in Hollywood. She's the kind of young woman who can talk about doing projects with Oprah Winfrey and Whitney Houston.

And she's also someone who knows the value of education. Her career might be in full effect, but that's not stopping her going to college, attending Pepperdine University, Malibu, where she's studying psychology. Okay, she's not your ordinary student, dashing here, there, and everywhere to get things done, but she's taking care of business, juggling all to make it work. Sometimes that means having to live on McDonald's, but that's okay—she can handle that quite easily, since it's one of her favorites.

The future is about as golden as it can get. This fall will see a Brandy comic book from DC comics. She's going to be doing an advertising campaign for Candie's shoes. She sang at the opening of the 1998 Goodwill Games. Everywhere you turn, everything is coming up Brandy.

When she has the time, she still likes to hang at the malls—although time is getting harder and harder to find these days. Someday, though, it will all settle down a little, someday when she meets someone—Brandy is currently very single since her breakup with Wayna Morris, and in no hurry for another long-term romance—settles down, marries, and has kids of her own.

But that is all well down the road. For now she has enough on her plate, singing, acting, just being Brandy, the teen icon, the Princess of R&B. And a normal, good person on top of everything else.

She's got it all. She's earned it. Just by being herself,

she's one of the best role models around: sweet, honest, and totally genuine. It's hard to find anyone to say that about, let alone someone in show business. She's just the coolest.

one

❦

Mississippi has never been one of the richest states in the Union. Quite the opposite—it's one of the poorest. The western boundary is the mighty Mississippi River, heading south from Memphis. The famous Highway 51 runs almost parallel to the water, going through Clarksdale and the Mississippi Delta at the north end of the state, which isn't really a delta at all, but the home of some of the most famous bluesmen America has ever produced—names like Robert Johnson and Muddy Waters.

At the southern end of the state, the land reaches the Gulf of Mexico, where Biloxi does solid business as a port. Slightly to the west, however, the state line jogs north and then west as it borders Louisiana. This is the deep south, pretty much as far as you can get, where the main industries in the rolling hills are timber and oil, and the weather fills with humidity in the summer.

It's in this area, on Highway 98, just east of the intersection with Highway 51, that the town of McComb stands. About twenty miles north of the Louisiana border, there's little to distinguish it from many other small towns dotted around the South.

By Mississippi standards, with some twelve thousand residents it's a relatively good size. It's fairly isolated, but still only about one hundred miles from the state capital of Jackson, or Hattiesburg, farther east on 98. And Baton Rouge, Louisiana, is even closer than that.

Like so many small towns, not a great deal seems to happen in McComb. Many of the families, both black and white, have been in the area for decades, sometimes even centuries. People know each other, always have, and know each other's business.

Gospel music has long been part of the Southern religious tradition, the choirs lifting their voices enthusiastically in praise of God. The choirs are important parts of any church, the best voices in the congregation rehearsing and working together. In the late 1970s, a young man named Willie Norwood got a job as the director of the church choir in Brookhaven, Mississippi, a town some twenty miles north of his home in McComb. Musical, and a good singer, he was the perfect man for the job, and it was one that suited him.

Willie was married to a woman named Sonja, who had a good job of her own as the manager at the local H&R Block office, in charge of people preparing tax returns. Both Willie and Sonja were college graduates, products of the sixties and the Civil Rights movement that had seemed to tear the South apart for a while.

For generations the stifling legacy of slavery had lain over the life of African-Americans in the southern states. The Civil Rights movement helped to slowly change that, to begin to bring racial equality.

Willie and Sonja Norwood benefitted from all that. It didn't mean they'd turned their back on their heritage, however, far from it. Just like their parents and grandparents before them, they were both religious people, raised in the church, which continued to be their spiritual home, and for Willie his place of work, too.

When, in 1978, Sonja discovered she was pregnant, the couple was overjoyed. They wanted children to make their home complete, to fill out the family. They even had names picked out—a boy would be William, Jr., and a girl would be Brandy.

However full of anticipation they were, nothing could match up to the reality, and when Brandy Norwood was born on February 11, 1979, in McComb, the event was like magic, a true gift from God. Sonja was twenty-seven and Willie twenty-nine.

But there seemed to be something even more special about her daughter to Sonja Norwood. All new babies seem remarkable to their mothers, but Sonja had a sense of something incredible for the future about the little girl she was holding.

"I know Brandy was going to be a star the day she was born," Sonja said. "I told the doctor that he has just delivered a star and that she was going to be something one day."

How could she know? Was it a sixth sense? Or just wishful thinking on the part of an exhausted new mom? The conversation was forgotten by everyone except Sonja, who remained convinced that Brandy possessed something that other girls didn't. Exactly what it was, or when she'd know, remained to be seen.

Life returned to normal in the Norwood house, or as

normal as things could get with a young baby around. Willie was working at the church, rehearsing the choir and preparing the music, and eventually Sonja returned to her job at H&R Block. Every Sunday the family would go to the church up in Brookhaven, dressed in their best clothes. Sonja would sit in the pew, tending little Brandy, as Willie conducted the choir.

Brandy grew quickly and very precociously. Like every kid, she went through the crawling stage, investigating everything, then walking, falling over a lot at first, then becoming steadier on her feet. There were so many big moments for Sonja and Willie—their little girl's first smile, her first step, and eventually her first word.

There was always music around the house. It was simply a part of life there, and a part of life that seemed to be in the air all over the South. So it was as no surprise to the Norwoods when their daughter began singing. After all, kids did sing, whether it was the nursery rhymes they used to help her learn, the lullabies to send her to sleep, TV theme songs, records she heard. Brandy just seemed to be able to soak them all up and sing them back. What was surprising was how well she could sing, and how powerfully. It didn't seem like the voice of a two-year-old, but much more mature, that seemed to come from . . . well, people didn't know where. Except for Sonja, who began to understand the premonition she'd had when Brandy was born.

Brandy seemed to love the music at church, too, and was soon singing along with the congregation on the hymns and songs. It was apparent to people besides her proud parents that the girl had something special, and

Willie was persuaded to let her sing with the choir as its youngest member.

It didn't take long to realize that Brandy was a standout, even among the strong choir that Willie had. Within a few months, she was a featured soloist, much to the pride and satisfaction of her parents.

Brandy seemed to be a natural performer, the kind of little girl who just lit up in front of an audience, and who, in turn, could completely light up and captivate a crowd. It didn't seem like a toddler singing, but someone else, someone much more grown-up, self-assured, someone who belonged in front of people.

From time to time, Willie and Sonja would discuss the possibilities for their daughter, but there were more pressing matters at hand. Sonja was pregnant again, about to give birth to the couple's second child, and for the moment that was more important than anything else. When Willie, Jr. was born, the family felt complete, full. They were happy, their babies growing well, Sonja and Willie both fulfilled in their jobs and their lives.

Once they'd established the routine with their new infant, talk returned to what they could do about their daughter. That she *needed* to be in front of people, singing, was quite obvious. And they also knew that just being in a church choir wasn't going to be enough for her. Sonja was still very firm in her belief that the girl would be a star. She was a lovely child, with big brown eyes and high cheekbones, full of personality without ever being sassy—one thing Sonja and Willie insisted on was bringing their kids up right.

If she was ever going to do something, it wouldn't be in McComb or Brookhaven, or anywhere in Mississippi, for that matter. They could have photographs made and send them to agents who handled young talent, but that wasn't going to help unless they lived somewhere else, a place where Brandy could work.

At first the talks were more theory than anything else, but soon Willie and Sonja realized they were quite serious, that Brandy did have a future as a singer and performer, and that they needed to become serious if they were going to do anything about it. They'd need to move, and there were only two possible places—New York or Los Angeles, the centers of the music and entertainment business.

Wherever they went, it was a big decision, a huge step. It would mean leaving friends and family, everything the Norwoods had ever known, and being completely on their own. It would also mean leaving the South, which took a lot of consideration.

In the South, small-town life seemed to move along at a slightly slower pace than the rest of the world. The days weren't filled with the clatter and bustle of people and cars hurrying here and there. There was time to actually *enjoy* life, to stop and smell the roses, to enjoy that piece of pie for dessert without having to rush off to a meeting. In some ways, leaving all that would be the biggest problem.

Sonja and Willie talked and talked, and finally realized they could talk forever and do nothing, or they could come to a decision. If Brandy was going to do anything, moving was the answer. But where—California or New York?

For so many Southerners, the idea of New York seemed horrible. The big, big city, where the people had a reputation for being rude, with all its crime and pollution. Was that really where they wanted to live after spending so many years surrounded by trees and green hills? Not really.

Of course, California didn't seem that much more attractive. Los Angeles might have had sunshine and palm trees, but it also had a reputation for clogged freeways, people driving everywhere, a place where image was everything and substance meant nothing, where everything was fake.

California did offer something New York couldn't, though—good weather. Maybe there were mudslides and always the threat of an earthquake, but there was also lots of sunshine, very little humidity, and no freezing cold and mountains of snow in the winter. New York had those, and almost tropical summers, with plenty of humidity. That was okay in a small town, where you could sit in the shade on a porch and sip some iced tea, but in the city there was no relief.

A lot also depended on where Willie and Sonja could find work. They might be going to help make Brandy into a star, but they still needed money to live on. Sonja's job was relatively transportable, since H&R Block had offices all over the country, and their busy season was really only from January to the end of April each year, at tax time. Wille, though, needed a church to be able to perform his job, so he had to discover what vacancies existed around Southern California, and begin applying.

With his background and his enthusiasm, it wasn't too long before he had an offer from a church in the perfect location—Carson, California.

It was a community of some 50,000 people in the San Fernando Valley, right on the edge of Long Beach, to the south of Los Angeles, with the big city still close enough to be accessible. Carson itself still had something of a small town feeling, even though it was really a part of the huge L.A. metropolis. And Redondo Beach, with sand and surf, was only ten miles away—no distance at all.

It all seemed ideal. Willie couldn't have asked for anything better. So when the offer arrived, he quickly accepted it. So, in 1983, the Norwoods began the massive task of packing and relocating.

It all seemed so final, going through their belongings and figuring out what to keep and transport across the country, and what to just leave behind. Everything seemed to hold a memory. And then there were all the family and friends who kept stopping by the house. For the kids it wouldn't be bad—Brandy had some friends in McComb, but she would adapt easily enough, and Willie, Jr. was so young that he wouldn't even really notice the difference. But for Sonja and Willie, every day made them realize how big a step this was. Even the excitement of a new job and a new life couldn't completely stop the sadness of leaving everything they'd ever known.

Eventually, though, they were ready. The moving truck was full, and had already set off for the west. There was nothing left but final goodbyes and promises to keep in touch, to see people soon. The kids were packed in the car, along with everything they'd need for the journey. Willie turned the key, pulled the gearshift into drive, and the Norwoods headed off for a new life.

The scenery changed as they moved across Louisiana and into Texas, the green hills giving way to a dryness that just seemed to get drier and drier. West Texas semmed to be parched, almost desert, the air conditioning in the car working overtime to keep the family cool. At night they'd stop at motels to rest, Willie's eyes weary from a day of watching the road, and the family would eat out at a diner. Then, next morning, it was back in the car and onto the road, neither of the children quite understanding why they were on this journey that never seemed to end. New Mexico had the towering mesas and more desert, the history of the Native American tribes up in the hills, the people who'd been here before whites or blacks.

Phoenix was the first huge city they'd come across on the trip. So clean, with the sky so blue, it seemed a good omen for things to come. From Arizona, the road took them across the Mojave Desert, and through the Joshua Tree National Park, before climbing up into the San Bernadino Mountains, higher than Brandy or Willie, Jr. had ever been in their lives, several thousand feet in the air, before descending on the other side, into the valley, and out toward the sea, and what was going to be home, on Interstate 10.

Every mile seemed to become more and more built up, with houses, stores, malls. And the traffic was unlike anything they'd encountered, each road so busy, Willie concerned with directions, finding his way through all the unfamiliar streets and roads to Carson. The signs kept coming ... Downey, Willowbook, Compton ... until finally they reached the exit for Carson. There things seemed to calm a little, like an oasis, and they could relax, as Willie searched for the house they'd rented that would become home. Finally he pulled up in front of the place. They'd arrived. A new life was waiting for them.

Adjusting to life in a new place is never easy. Even the basic small things, like running to the grocery store, become harder. It took a little while for the Norwoods to settle into Carson. The city was friendly, there was no problem with that; it was simply a case of learning everything anew.

Once the family had settled in, they had to wonder what to do about Brandy and getting her a career. It wasn't as if Willie and Sonja were experienced stage parents. They really had no idea how to go about it, other than the fact that they wanted to approach everything cautiously. Whatever happened would happen in its own sweet time. And that was just fine.

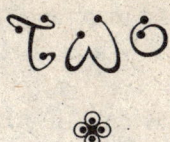

Two

For a long time, nothing much did happen. A good education came before everything else, both for Brandy and Willie, Jr. That was what Willie and Sonja firmly believed—family, education, church were the cornerstones of a good life.

As she grew, Brandy sang at all the talent shows, and attended open-call auditions with her mother, who believed in her even when she came home without any kind of small part. Sonja had known that her daughter was going to be a star, and she was still absolutely certain of the fact.

One immediate problem was that there were lots of kids in Los Angeles who could act and sing and were very cute. Competition for each child role was tremendous. With success, Brandy could get an agent, and things would become a little bit easier. But that wouldn't happen until she achieved some success. It seemed like a vicious circle.

And there weren't that many parts for African-American girls. Things were slightly better than they had been, but color weighted the dice against her.

Singing remained Brandy's great love, and her biggest talent. Coached by her father, her voice continued to improve. But her biggest inspiration came in 1985, when she was six, and heard Whitney Houston for the very first time on the radio.

The song was "Saving All My Love For You," (which was a cover of a 1978 Marilyn McCoo and Billy Davis, Jr., album track), and it would become a massive hit, topping the charts in both America and England. Whitney's voice struck a deep chord in Brandy.

"I want to be just like her," she told her parents. Considering that Whitney not only had the Number One single, but also the Number One album, that was going to take a lot of doing, but it told the Norwoods that their daughter hadn't lost any ambition.

And Whitney was the perfect inspiration for a young performer. She'd started out as a backing singer for people like Chaka Khan and Lou Rawls, then carved a career as a model, appearing on the covers of *Glamour* and *Seventeen*, as well as being an actress with roles on the TV sitcoms *Silver Spoons* and *Gimme A Break*—all before she became a solo performer.

Then, when she hit big, she hit it *really* big. Between 1986 and 1990, Whitney had nine hit singles—eight of them traveling all the way to the magical Number One slot—and three multi-platinum albums. Her second album, *Whitney*, was a landmark, the first album ever by a female singer to debut at Number One on the *Billboard* album charts. On top of that were all her awards, winning everything but a Grammy.

She was an African-American woman, a role model to a generation, who was breaking all manner of records, and would continue to do so. Her first film, *The Bodyguard* (1992) would do tremendous business, and one of Whitney's songs from the soundtrack, "I Will Always Love You" would set yet another new record, staying at Number One for fourteen weeks (although that would eventually be broken by Boyz II Men and Mariah Carey, duetting on "One Sweet Day," which would hold the top position for sixteen weeks).

On top of that, Whitney came from a church background; her mother was gospel and soul singer Cissy Houston. Could there have been a more ideal model for Brandy, someone who'd done everything she wanted to do herself, and had succeeded so well at it?

The young Brandy bought all Whitney's records, and studied them all carefully, learning from them, copying at first, then taking things to use as part of her own style.

With each year she was entering more talent shows and beginning to win them. Her voice continued to grow remarkably, and onstage she'd become a seasoned performer, one who could handle an audience, who knew how to keep the crowd with her. Her confidence had grown.

California was proving to be good to the Norwoods. Willie enjoyed his job as the church's music direcotr, and Sonja had found another branch of H&R Block to manage. The kids were growing well, and Willie, Jr. seemed to be following in his big sister's footsteps as a singer and performer.

But it was Brandy who seemed to be the focus of attention, older, and slowly making things happen. Even so, it just wasn't easy. In a town crowded with talent, Brandy was still learning, still improving. Sonja, too, was learning, about the business and how to make it work for her as the manager looking after her children's affairs.

There were very few acting roles open for African-American kids, and those seemed to go, time and again, to a select few who'd already managed to make their mark. Breaking into show business from that end seemed almost impossible, so Sonja concentrated her efforts on music, which was where Brandy's greatest talent seemed to lie anyway.

That route wasn't much easier. There was very little market for child performers. They were looked at as novelties in the music business, and not taken seriously, although Brandy had a voice well beyond her years. It was a frustrating time for everyone, but for the moment there was no option but to lay the groundwork, to groom Brandy and make her as professional as poosible, and wait for the future.

Of course, Brandy and Sonja pursued every lead, entered all the talent shows, and answered all the calls for open auditions. At some point, something would lead somewhere.

While her life was focused on all this, it didn't mean that Brandy totally lived for it. With school and her friends, she also had a really normal life, hanging out, listening to records, going to the mall, doing all the things that girls do, dishing, going to McDonald's. It was just that she also had this extra element in her life that her friends didn't. She was driven, but that didn't mean that she couldn't also have some fun.

The Norwoods lived a quiet, middle-class life. Not as rich as the Huxtable family on television's *Cosby* show, they were still comfortable, with aspirations for themselves and for their kids. Neither Brandy nor Willie, Jr. wanted for things. The house in Carson was well-furnished, Brandy's room with its Whitney Houston poster on the wall.

By now it was the late 1980s, and the family had been living in Southern California for several years, without any notable success for Brandy. She'd won plenty of talent shows, and her abilities had been praised, but none of it had led to paying gigs, to anything solid. She'd sing anywhere she could, anywhere she was asked, but the big break was proving very elusive. How long could it stay that way, she wondered.

The change—or the start of the change—came in 1989. It seemed like another open audition, this one for a movie. Sonja drove Brandy down, and went in with her, joining all the other mothers and children waiting there. So many faces were familiar from other auditions, and they stopped to chat to people they knew. Brandy knew the routine all too well by now—she'd have a couple of minutes to show what she could do, and that would be all. If she was really, really lucky, there might be a callback for a second audition. Otherwise she'd hear nothing more. But she had faith in herself, because her parents had faith in her. They knew she'd make it eventually, and it never occured to her to question that. It just seemed that she'd been put on earth to entertain, that it was her whole reason for being.

Finally she was called, went up on the stage, and performed for the people she couldn't see. It was always nerve-wracking to know someone was out there, but not knowing who or where. She finished and walked off. It was over, and she wouldn't have to think about it until the next time.

Except that within a couple of days she received a callback, and after that another, until she learned that she'd won her first part! Granted, it was small, but it meant she'd crossed that boundary and actually achieved something concrete. More than that, it was in a movie that was going to be fairly high-profile, whose name would undoubtedly be remembered—if anyone could pronounce it.

Arachnophobia might not have had a star-studded cast (John Goodman, of *Roseanne* fame was probably the biggest name), but it would have good special effects, some surprisingly good acting, and strong direction from a newcomer named Frank Marshall, who just happened to be a friend and producer of Steven Spielberg.

Arachnophobia means a fear of spiders, which most people have to a greater or lesser extent, and the movie of the same name really played on that. The killer spiders from South America migrated to California, mated with local spiders, and began terrorizing a small town. Jeff Daniels, playing the town's spider-hating doctor, teamed up with Goodman the exterminator to battle the problem.

It was hardly high art, but it was grand entertainment, with some remarkably convincing special effects to keep audiences on the edge of their seats.

For Brandy, just landing the role in *Arachnophobia* made her feel like a success. When she reported to the set, her few lines memorized and already gone over fifty or more different ways, she felt on top of the world. This is what it was like, and this is what it would be like for her in the future. Just being there made her feel like a star, although, in truth, she still had a long way.

Filmed during the summer of 1989, it was a great experience for Brandy Norwood. For her few days of filming, she observed and listened, soaking in everything she could. Everything offered her a chance to learn, to become better at the things she did. She'd never expected that her first break would come as an actress, but that was the way the dice had fallen, and she was going to take advantage of it.

She'd tried her hand as an actress simply because it increased the opportunities for her, although she still thought of herself primarily as a singer. Being here, though, she began to realize that it might be possible to combine the two, to have *two* careers. There was absolutely no sense in limiting yourself—you were the only person you hurt if you did that.

When *Arachnophobia* appeared in 1990, it did surprisingly well at the box office, drawing in audiences all through the summer, particularly for the scary effects, making the film into a hit. Of course, with everything going on, very few people ever noticed that Brandy was in there, too, with her three lines of dialogue. Somehow, though, when she saw herself up on her the screen, and heard her own voice through the speakers, the fact that few people would ever know that was her didn't matter. Getting this far had given her the drive to go a lot further.

Having the drive and actually getting the roles were two different things, however. At eleven years old, Brandy was really in transition. No longer was she a cute little girl. But she wasn't a teenager yet, either, and there just wasn't much for that in-between phase.

The idea of acting had come on very strong in her mind, and quite understandably, but she wasn't ignoring her singing. She was still working with her father, still entering talent shows, and trying to make it. But the problem was that she still wasn't old enough to be taken seriously. With one big exception. The Norwoods had been involved with the Brotherhood Crusade, and in 1990, Brandy was named Darling of the Brotherhood Crusade. Along with the title, she had the opportunity to sing onstage, at the festivities organized to honor the Crusade's Man of the Year, Arsenio Hall, who then had one of America's hottest talk show. The song? A version of Whitney's hit, "The Greatest Love of All." Along with the movie role, it was a highlight of her life so far.

But, in spite of that, it would be a couple of years before anything else really happened for her professionally, and once again, that would be a movie.

Demolition Man, which appeared in 1993, although it was filmed the year before, was a big sci-fi action movie, a vehicle for Sylvester Stallone, playing a cryogenically frozen cop pursuing a criminal (Wesley Snipes). And, being a Stallone film, there was no shortage of violence, even in the future when pursuer and pursued were thawed into an ideal society, where virtual sex was the only sex, and everyone was PC and orderly.

As with *Arachnophobia*, Brandy auditioned for a small part, and after a couple of callbacks, won the role. It wasn't the kind of film that interested her, and certainly not one Willie and Sonja would let their daughter see, but there was a difference between the personal and professional, most certainly at this stage.

Being on the set did give Brandy a chance to see one

of the major black stars, Wesley Snipes, doing his stuff, and once again, she learned a great deal simply be being there, and keeping her eyes and ears open. She was drinking it all in, learning every moment, although, since she only had a few lines of dialogue, her time there was very limited, only a few days.

The fact that she'd managed to get two parts was tremendously encouraging. She couldn't help but feel that things were beginning to come together for her as she entered her teens. She went into a studio to record for the first time, too. Her parents believed that the time was finally right to try and find a record deal. Certainly she'd spent enough time paying her dues in all those talent contests and small gigs. Her voice was adult enough to be taken seriously, and although she definitely looked like a teen, she didn't look like a little girl any longer.

On top of being on a film set, this was like paradise to Brandy, to sing with a band, to be able to hear herself on the headphones during the playback of a track and *really* know the way her voice sounded. To hear the musicians, and the way the tracks all came together, then the mixdown, which took the raw material from her and the musicians and refined it into a finished product. This was magic, and it was *her* magic.

It wasn't just a case of making a tape, sending it to record companies, and hoping that someone liked what they heard and signed her to a contract. The business just didn't work that way. What Brandy needed first was a manager or a lawyer, someone who could approach the record company on her behalf, who knew people there, and could get her tape listened to.

All those years of singing for nothing had paid off.

Brandy's name had become a little known, enough to interest a few management companies. No one was offering her any money yet, but people were at least interested in representing her.

Still, none of that translated into a record deal of any kind—yet. And at first, it didn't seem as if anyone was drumming up interest. But the Norwoods continued to work their contacts. After looking after Brandy's career—and now also Willie, Jr.'s as he began acting, they'd come to know people. There had been guests at the weddings where Brandy had sung, people who knew people, and every lead could be followed up. One of them translated into something very prestigious—a spot on *Showtime at the Apollo*, filmed at the famous Harlem theater. It was a real coup for Brandy to be on there, without a record contract, and a true sign that she would be going places.

And there was another avenue—being a backup singer to a group. Being a backup singer certainly wasn't what Brandy had in mind for herself, but it was another opportunity, a chance to acquire more professional experience.

The Norwoods were put in touch with another group, one that was really hitting its stride. Immature, as they were known, had a record deal with Virgin, one of the big labels. They were three boys, just a little older than Brandy—Marques "Batman" Houston, Jerome "Romeo" Jones, and Kelton "LDB" Kessee. They sang R&B, not a million miles removed from Color Me Badd or Boyz II Men, and were based in Los Angeles. They needed a female singer to help fill out their sound, and because of the connection and the age, Brandy seemed like the natural choice.

When their album, *On Our Worst Behavior*, appeared in 1992, it immediately sold well, and the single, "Tear It Up," which was featured on a movie soundtrack, also began to get radio play and some chart action. For shows in the Los Angeles area, Brandy appeared onstage with them. It was strictly in the background, but getting a tiny bit closer to the kind of big time she was seeking for herself, and another line to put on her resume. Other singers had gotten their professional start singing backup—Mariah Carey, for instance, who'd worked behind Brenda K. Starr for a little while in the late 1980s—and gone on to great careers, so why shouldn't it also work for Brandy?

Slowly, very slowly, it seemed to be coming together. Things were changing.

One of the biggest changes came that September, in the fall of 1992, when Brandy enrolled as a freshman at Hollywood High Performing Arts Center. She'd had to audition to be accepted at the high school, but she'd passed with flying colors. Being there seemed like being part of *Fame*. The students were all actors, singers, musicians, or dancers. As well as academic classes, the kids would have plenty of chances to pratice their particular talents, and the teachers would help by sending them out on auditions.

In drama class, it seemed like most of the students were being encouraged by the teacher, who would send them to audition for parts. But Brandy wasn't included in that list, and she couldn't understand why. In her own mind she had every bit as much talent as the others, as much drive and passion for acting.

"One day I asked, 'Why aren't you sending me out on calls?' and she said, 'Because you're not drop-dead gorgeous.' My heart just dropped," Brandy said.

While appearance mattered, beauty should never have been a factor. It was supposed to be about talent, not looks. And beauty, of course, was in the eye of the beholder. What one person considered ugly, another might find wonderful.

It was an ill-considered remark on the part of the teacher, and one which did nothing to encourage Brandy, but having come so far, she wasn't about to give up. If anything, it strengthened her determination to prove her teacher wrong, to show that she could make it, no matter how she looked, or the color of her skin, or anything else someone might be able to find fault with, if they really wanted to. Her parents believed in her, and Brandy believed in herself. With faith, and help from God, she'd make it and show everyone.

Her demo tape was circulating, and by the beginning of 1993 was starting to gather some interest from a number of labels. It was as if all the groundswell, all the work Brandy and her parents had put in, might finally pay off. A tape could only tell people from the Artist and Repertoire departments (the real talent scouts, who were responsible for signing new artists) so much, however. What they really wanted was to see Brandy perform, to get a sense of her onstage, and make sure she was as good as she seemed, since studio tricks could do a lot to make a singer sound better than she really was.

The next step was to organize a showcase for her, where she could sing for all the suits, or label executives, strut her stuff, and show everything she'd learned over the last ten years in Los Angeles.

Now it was all up to her.

THREE

The showcase was set for early in the year. Which meant that, apart from schoolwork, Brandy had to rehearse intensely with the musicians who'd be backing her; nothing could go wrong on this, no bum notes, no forgotten lyrics. Everything had to be perfect.

She was used to being onstage, to having an audience when she sang, but the thought of this one made her nervous. So much rested upon it. If it went well, it could lead to a big record deal, and after that the sky was the limit. If she blew it... well, that didn't bear thinking about.

As the big day drew closer, she was more and more nervous, and her parents tried to calm her down. It would be good to have the adrenaline flowing, to draw the best out of their daughter, but they didn't want her paralyzed by fear.

Sonja and Willie Norwood had been talking to the people at Atlantic Records, who'd shown a great deal of interest in Brandy's tape. But, like the other labels, they wanted to see her live before they made a final decision. However, Ron Shapiro, who was Atlantic's executive vice president and general manager, had a very strong feeling about this new act.

"From the second I laid eyes on her, I knew she was going to be a superstar," he said. "If you look into her eyes, you're gone. It's like a sweet charisma that's also provocative."

The question was, could that "sweet charisma" come across onstage? While she'd be playing to people who were interested in her, these were folks from the record industry who'd seen it all before, and who weren't easily convinced. They were jaded, and something had to be very special to keep their attention. In many ways they were more interested in talking business than in doing business.

Backstage, Brandy was collecting her thoughts, focusing on her songs, warming up her voice, and putting herself into the moment that lay ahead. She knew how much was riding on it, but tried to put that out of her mind. If she dwelt on it, her nerves would reappear. Instead, she let peaceful thoughts flood in, things to make her smile, memories, dreams, images of a good future. This was her night, and she was going to be in complete control of it. The people out there had come to see her, and she'd make sure they were *hers*, and went away thinking of her.

Then it was time to walk on and take the evening. The house lights dimmed and she entered and the band waited behind her. As the first song began, everyone who'd been talking before seemed to start a new conversation. There was no way she could sing with all that going on around her, distracting. She motioned to the band to stop, and in a second there was just the buzz of conversation.

"She said, 'You're being rude,'" recalled Ron Shapiro. "And I panicked. And the crowd silenced. But then she started singing, and they listened. And she won them over."

It was a daring thing to do. In that second she could have lost them completely. It could have seemed totally amateurish, like a girl who felt she didn't have any hope of controlling them. Instead, it came across as a young woman demanding respect, and that was what she was given as she ran through her set.

The songs were what she did best, some soft R&B, with a couple of ballads to show that she had the range and ability to handle them properly. Having taken everything into her own hands, she owned the audience for the half-hour she was in the spotlight. They watched her and listened to her. She had magic about her, and it all worked perfectly, exactly the way she'd hoped it would. It wasn't a high school freshman they were watching, but a young woman with a strong voice and a mature way of putting a song across, as well as the type of charisma that came along all too rarely. She wasn't just another singer, that was obvious; she was a star in the making.

"Brandy stood out," said Darryl Williams, who was then the head of A&R for Atlantic Records, and attending the showcase with Shapiro. "She was just energetic and had an incredible voice for a fourteen-year-old."

When she finished, the applause was far more than polite, but Brandy barely heard it. Backstage, she felt like a wreck. What had she *done*, telling all those people to shut up? Okay, they'd quieted down, but those were the people who could make her future. Sonja and Willie were waiting for her, absolutely ecstatic. She'd done it, she'd completely knocked them out. Already there was a buzz going around the club about her. People wanted to talk, they wanted to do business and make records—with her.

As the adrenaline from the biggest performance of her life started to slip away, Brandy Norwood just felt tired. She'd put everything into the evening, almost as if she'd been another person up there. She'd given it her best shot, and she knew it her heart that it had gone as well as anything she'd ever done. Now there was nothing more she could do. It was out of her hands. She was the singer. If she'd impressed anyone, then her parents would hear about it. If not, well, she had nothing to regret. She couldn't have done any better.

After the high of performing, going back to school was a letdown. She sang and acted there, and hung out with other kids who did, but it just wasn't the same. There wasn't the same thrill about it, but that was only to be expected.

Meanwhile, behind the scenes, things were moving. The Norwoods continued to talk to Atlantic, who were becoming very serious about Brandy recording for them.

There was a lot more to a recording contract than a simple signature on a piece of paper (although, since she was still only fourteen, Brandy wasn't yet old enough to sign anyway). It was all about getting the best deal, and in Los Angeles, the land of the deal, that was an art form. On behalf of the artist, it was a case of negotiating the best advance—the money paid when the contract was signed—the best royalty rate. For the company, it was about hopefully making as much profit as possible. So everyone was jockeying for position.

Negotiations could last a long time, but it was in everyone's interests to strike a bargain sooner rather than later, while there was still a lot of buzz, and it was obvious that a number of companies were interested. Right now Brandy's position was strong. Her showcase had been *so* good that it wasn't just Atlantic who was after her—they were just the leading contenders.

Finally, it all came to a head. For the Norwoods, Atlantic seemed like the best choice. The money was right, but more than that, they were one of the very big labels, part of the WEA group, with plenty of clout, and the ability to promote their artists properly. Atlantic had been the home to some great music in the past, artists like Ray Charles and the Queen of Soul herself, Aretha Franklin. They had a real commitment to the music.

The deal was done. Brandy was going to be recording her debut album for Atlantic. She'd made it, and made it as a singer. She could be the new Whitney Houston. More importantly, she could be the first Brandy. It was certainly something to tell the teacher who hadn't sent her out on auditions. She might not be "drop-dead gorgeous" but she could still make it ahead of a lot of those who were.

Getting a deal was just the beginning of things. It wasn't a case of going straight into a studio, making an album, and having it out the next week. Life could never be that simple. The first hurdle was selecting songs and producers to work with Brandy, and that was all handled by

Darryl Wilson, who took on the title of exexutive producer for the record, which essentially meant overseeing everything that happened.

In many cases, the producers of different tracks would also be their writers, and often the people playing the keyboards, and sequencing the drum machines.

Once the producers and the songs had been selected, which usually meant winnowing down from literally hundreds of tunes and names to find the ones that would work best, everything went into preproduction. During that time Brandy was spending all her time in the studio, making demo versions of the songs for everyone to listen to and come up with the definitive arrangements which would end up on the CD. Background vocals had to be worked out, and all the basic studio problems overcome.

Throughout this time she was still attending Hollywood High Performing Arts Center, doing well in her classes—she remained a straight-A student—and going out on auditions.

One chance in particular seemed good, a television sitcom that was being cast. The producers needed an African-American girl to play the younger daughter of the lead. Not that there weren't plenty of young African-American actresses around, but it did cut down on the competition. Waiting for her chance to audition, Brandy and Sonja saw plenty of familiar faces. That a new show about blacks might end up on television was good news in and of itself for everyone there. Even if they didn't get this role, there might be something a little down the line. And if it did well, it would spawn imitators, which would offer more opportunities in the future.

For now, though, this was the one. Brandy approached

her audition with a lot more confidence. Right now, with her record deal, she didn't need this role. She loved to act, but more than anything she knew she should be focusing on her music. That nonchalance and attitude colored her performance, and obviously impressed people. A couple of days later, she received a callback for another audition.

It was impossible *not* to see all the irony in this. For years she felt like she'd been banging her head against a brick wall, with very little to show for her efforts apart from two tiny film roles, over so quickly that you missed them if you blinked, and now everyone seemed to want her at the same time. If it wasn't so funny, it would have made her cry.

The callback went ever better than the initial audition. Over the next two weeks she went back again and again, until finally she was offered the role.

It was unbelievable! After years of nothing, now she had too much on her plate. She had to make a choice. Either she could do both things, which would stretch her to the limit, or she could just concentrate on her singing.

At this stage, to turn down any serious offer would have been stupid. Brandy knew it, and so did Sonja, who was now officially her manager. For now, the only involvement with this show was to make a pilot episode to show to the networks, and hope someone picked it up. All too often, pilots never even saw the light of day on television. Until it was picked up—if it was picked up at all—there was absolutely no guarantee of a series. Even if it *was* picked up, the network could ask for changes in characters. No, it was better to take it, and put in the work for a while, and hope for the best. At the very worst, it would be another entry on Brandy's resume.

Thea, as the show was named, starred Thea Vidale as a widow trying hard to raise her children in Houston, Texas, holding everything together while maintaining a full-time job in a grocery store. This wasn't the in-your-face humor that characterized so many of the black shows to television, particularly those on the FOX network, but more the good family values that had been such a part of *The Cosby Show*, all in a blue-collar environment. It wanted to be funny, positive, and real.

As originally written, Thea was the mother of five—three sons and two daughters. By the time the pilot was shot, however, that had been reduced to four kids, Jarvis Turrell II (Adam Jefferies), Jerome (Jason Weaver), James (Brenden Jefferson), and Danesha (Brandy, using her full name of Brandy Norwood).

In many ways, Brandy was the least experienced professionally in the whole cast, enjoying her first television role—at least, she would be if someone picked it up. But she was too busy to be nervous about things, trying to divide her time and her concentration between the pilot, work on her album, and school, and do the best she could on all three.

The fictional location for *Thea* might have been Houston, but everything on the pilot was shot on a soundstage in Los Angeles. It served as an introduction to Thea Turrell and her family. Of course, it was all about a conflict that had to be resolved. In this case, her middle son, Jerome, wanted to attend a video game tournament, but Thea didn't want to let him go. However, while she was at work, he convinced his older brother, Jarvis, that everything would be fine if he went. When Thea arrived home from work, and discovered what had happened, she went to the tournament herself to find Jerome, leaving Jarvis thinking that his brother would end up at dead man at their mother's hands. Instead, Thea let him stay on and even take part in the tournament.

Brandy didn't have a big role in the pilot, since it concentrated on the boys, but that didn't mean there was no work for her. Danesha still had to be introduced, she had to be at rehearsals and on the set. In many ways it wasn't too different from the films she'd been in, except everything moved more quickly. There wasn't the luxury of time and money for endless retakes.

And when she wasn't on the set or doing her schoolwork, she was back in the recording studio, finishing up pre-production for her record. This, she felt, was going to be the big one, even though she knew just how many records were released every year, and how few were actually successes. She believed in her talent, and so did Atlantic, which was spending quite a bit of money to make it all work for her. She was an investment for them, and she just hoped it would all pay off; in her heart she was sure it would. She *couldn't* have come so far just to fail.

Once the pilot was finished and edited, Brandy and her family went to a screening, and she had to admit, it looked good. It was funny, it was realistic, it managed to be sweet but still have a bit of an edge.

By then she wasn't the only one in the family who was acting. Her brother, Willie, Jr. was up for a role of his own, his first big break—on *The Sinbad Show*, which would be the comic Sinbad looking after a pair of kids. It would be something if they both ended up on series at the same time, something to make Willie and Sonja really proud of their offspring.

Thea was shown to the executives at ABC, and then everyone had to wait for a decision. For the people who made their livings as actors, it was a time of tension. If it was taken, it meant some serious money for as long as the show lasted. But until they knew, there was no opportunity to take on any other work. Time clicked by slowly, for everyone except Brandy. She had less at stake than everyone else. If the show didn't happen, she still had her album to make. If it did . . . well, then she'd be busy, very happily busy indeed.

Finally the call came. ABC had given *Thea* the green light, and a whole season of episodes, seventeen in all, had been ordered. Now it was a scramble to get to work, to have everything in place and some episodes already taped when the season began. Brandy was going to have a very full schedule.

FOUR

"When I signed my contract to record," Brandy remembered, "it was about three months before I got the part on the first TV show. The show was in the way for me at the time because singing came first. I'd be needed in the studio, but I'd have to say I couldn't go because I was taping the show!"

It wasn't a perfect situation, everyone knew that. But in the end it could have a huge payoff. Brandy's album was due for release the following year, in 1994. If *Thea* proved to be a hit, then Brandy's face would be well-known by the time the record appeared, which would certainly help sales. And if the record sold well, that would only help increase viewing figures for a second season of the sitcom.

That was looking ahead, of course. For now, Brandy was taking on an incredible amount of work. It was impossible to be on the set five days a week, in the studio, and go to school, so instead she received daily tutoring during filming breaks in *Thea*. Under California law, as a minor she could only be on the set for a total of ten-and-a-half hours a day. That seemed a lot, but when the adults were there between twelve and fourteen hours a day, her time, which included three hours' schooling, wasn't so great.

Then she'd be off to whichever recording studio she was supposed to be in that day—a total of six (Human Rhythm, Studio 56, EMI, Swing Bopulous, Aire L.A., and Larabee West) were used by the producers, all in different parts of Los Angeles. As soon as she finished her daily stint on *Thea* a car would be waiting to chauffeur her onward, to more work. At fourteen, she had plenty of energy and stamina, but it was still exhausting.

One of the brightest spots was that Brandy herself would be co-writing three of the tracks on the album. More interludes than full tracks—the longest wasn't quite a minute and a half—it still meant she'd have *some* creative input.

Keith Crouch, who'd be producing five tracks for the record, had a strong history in R&B production, having worked with people like Lalah Hathaway and Johnny Gill; the man knew how to write a hit and make it sound good, too. But there was also Arvel McClinton, Damon Thomas, and the team of Somthin' for the People (Jeffrey Young, Curtis "Sauce" Wilson, and Rochad Holiday) behind the control board for other tracks.

Trying to juggle everything, to be able to give her best at all times, proved to be good for Brandy.

"I grew up a lot," she explained. "I learned the responsibilities of having a job and having to take care of my own business. I learned to be focused. When it comes to singing, I've always been very focused."

One thing that the producers of *Thea* had been dicussing was using Brandy's vocal talents on the show, and having her sing occasionally. It would be good for the show, and for Brandy's character of Danesha Turrell, who was basically shy and quite serious about her schoolwork, boys, and chatting with girlfriends on the telephone. And it would make people aware that Brandy was a singer, which wouldn't hurt sales of her album when it appeared.

Thea premiered on ABC on Wednesday, September 8, 1993, a Wednesday night, following *Full House* and *Home Improvement*, two proven sitcoms. From the very beginning, its ratings were quite strong, crossing over from an African-American audience to become a real family comedy. That left everyone hopeful that more episodes would be ordered, another nine to make up a real complete season.

It all began with the pilot, which served as an introduction to the family. Then, a week later, it was Jerome who was in trouble again, this time because he was failing English, giving all his attention to trying to make the school basketball team. In an attempt to show him that education was more important than some hoops, Thea made sure he took the time do do a proper job on his book report (on the novel *To Kill A Mockingbird*) rather than practicing slam-dunks on the court. Jerome wasn't happy, and was even less happy when he didn't make the team. But everything came right when he ended up with an A on his report. Meanwhile, Danesha, who thought her family was hilarious, was trying—unsucessfully—to get them to act that way, so she could make a video to submit to *America's Funniest Home Videos*.

It was apparent from the first couple of episodes that Jerome and trouble seemed to go hand in hand, and in the third show he proved it again, planning a party for his friends around a boxing match on television while his mother was at night school, trying to better herself in a management training program. Needless to say, the best-laid plans of mice and Jeromes ended up going astray at the hands of Thea.

The next week, Jerome's fibbing was getting a little out of hand, which forced Thea to take things into her own hands (although not literally, of course) in order to keep him on the straight-and-narrow path.

Finally the spotlight moved away from Jerome and on to Jarvis, who was a good, if slightly naive, kid. Thea allowed him to join his uncle at a bachelor party, while she and her sister Lynette (Yvette Wilson) worked with their other sister to prepare her for the upcoming wedding. The highlight of the bachelor party was supposed to be a stripper, who was eventually persuaded to keep her clothes on in order to spare Jarvis. Being a gentleman, Jarvis even walked the stripper—he hadn't realized she was a stripper—to her bus. Unfortunately, he hadn't told anyone else where he was going, leaving his uncle thinking he'd run off somewhere. It all ended with everyone reunited for the wedding, with Brandy singing on the show for the first time, getting a chance to show the whole of America just how good her voice really was.

Thea was picking up in the ratings, and starting to do nearly as well as its lead-in shows. It was pre-empted a few times during the fall, but it seemed like everything was at one time or another.

In "Birthday Girl," the episode aired on November 3, 1993, Thea was celebrating her birthday, and none too happy about it. She was older, working too hard just to try and stay afloat while looking after the kids, and trying to see they were raised right. Her husband was dead, and she was alone in the world. It was up to the family to put a smile on her face, and make her realize all the things she should be grateful about. For the second time in two weeks (and, it turned out, the last time) Brandy sang on the show, this time to her fictional mother. Of course, they managed to make Thea happy again, and glad that she was getting a bit older, more patient, and able to cope with them all.

The next episode was Brandy's chance to shine. She and Leonard (Kenny Ford, Jr., who'd been a regular on Disney's *Kids Incorporated* before moving on to *Thea*) had spent the entire season trying to pretend they didn't really like each other. Danesha had been waiting for Leonard to admit that he liked her—it was so obvious that anyone could see it—but being a boy, he wasn't about to do make the first move. If anything was going to happen, she'd have to start it, something that wasn't too easy for a shy girl. Eventually she plucked up the courage. As soon as the words were out, he was willing to admit that he really liked her, too. It was first love, very sweetly done, without going over the top and being saccharine, but as real and tentative as anyone's first fumbling steps at romance. Their relationship would be an ongoing thread through the rest of the season's episodes.

By now it was mid-November, and no more episodes had been ordered. There was enough material to take them into February, given the way the schedule looked over the holidays. If *Thea* had been going to continue, they'd have heard by now, and been working furiously for the future. It was apparent to everyone that the show's days were numbered, and that sapped a lot of the enthusiasm from both cast and crew. Soon none of them would have a job, which meant that they all had to start looking around *now*, diverting some of their energy from the project at hand.

More than that, it left them depressed and bewildered. The show was doing well, not even halfway through its first year. There didn't seem to be any sense in dropping it, not when other shows on the schedule were much lower in the ratings. No one could understand it, but they had no choice but to accept. It was the network, ABC, that made the decisions.

The remaining episodes continued to do well in the ratings, and the cast gave it all they could, but it was difficult to be funny when you knew that in a few more weeks you'd be unemployed. As they worked ahead, taping shows that would be shown in a few weeks, their Christmas show, which was aired December 15, 1993, was actually filmed at the beginning of November, with nobody feeling particularly festive.

"Hair Today, Gone Tomorrow," which saw Thea having to give up an extra and necessary source of income—doing hair in her home—after a visit from the Board of Health—seemed heavy with premonitions of the future.

Early in the New Year, with 1994 barely started, they began work on the last show of *Thea*. The network had officially announced that the show would be ending, with some mid-season replacement thrown into its time slot, to sink or swim. The five days it took to rehearse and tape "Pie Queen and the Lone Duck" seemed endless to everyone involved. Over the last several months they'd come to know each other, and really become a family in many ways, even more so when they realized that their show didn't seem to have much chance of surviving.

Now it was all coming to an end, and there were very mixed feelings, both never wanting it to stop, and wanting it to be done *now*, so they could all move on with their lives.

For Brandy, who'd finally completed all the vocal overdubs on her album, it was especially difficult. This was her first series, and the fact that it was failing hurt deeply and personally. She had the drive to want to succeed at everything she did, for it all to be wonderful. She knew that she, and everyone else, had done good work on the show, that it was funny, and that people liked it. But somehow, that just didn't seem to be enough, and she couldn't understand it. Willie, Jr. was doing fine in *Sinbad*, and *Thea* had better ratings. It didn't make any sense. Just as she'd been able to focus entirely on acting, the rug was being pulled out from under her. Life was confusing.

The final episode aired, without much fanfare, on February 23, 1994. By then the wrap party was a memory, and everyone had gone their different ways. A few would meet again, but mostly they'd never see each other. It was sad, and it was impossible for Brandy not to feel an emptiness in her heart at losing this new family she'd just gained.

One big question was, why had the show been cancelled in the first place? Its ratings were strong enough to have continued—in fact, it was stronger than *Full House*, one of its lead-in shows.

The real reasons were never revealed, but there were plenty of rumors running around the cast. According to some sources, Jason Weaver (who played Jerome and who would go on to portray Marcus on the WB's *Smart Guy*), felt it had been cancelled in favor of a low-rated white show. Whether that was the case will never be known, and in a business dictated by ratings, it had to seem unlikely.

In some ways, the cancellation of *Thea* was helpful for Brandy. It meant she could concentrate on her album getting out there and promoting it to the fullest. The fact that she'd been on television and had a role in a series meant that some people at least knew her name—she wouldn't be a totally unknown quantity.

With a release date set, and her fifteenth birthday close at hand, Brandy could even relax a little bit, and indulge in her favorite occupation—shopping. She'd had so little time in the last nine months that it was a relief to be able to go and hang out at the mall and spend some money on clothes. And there were plenty of new labels to try. There was Polo, Tommy Hilfiger, all the shoes, everything to fill up her closet. She'd made some money and wanted to spend a little bit of it, as well as just chill there with her friends, whom she'd barely had time to see, let alone dish with.

She was still disappointed about *Thea*, but there was plenty ahead of her. Having heard the completed album, she was excited about the future. Singing still meant so much more to her than acting. Hearing herself made her feel proud of what she'd managed to achieve, and she knew her parents were also proud of her. They'd made big sacrifices to get her where she was, and Willie, Jr., who was now known in the family by his nickname Ray J., to his place on television. Life was very cool. As she waited for her mother to pick her up, surrounded by almost more bags than she could carry, she had every reason to feel pleased with herself.

At the same time, she was a little nervous. She was happy with the album, and she knew the label was, that they were going to push it, but it depended on a lot of things outside her control. She had a video to do—would MTV play it? Would radio play the first single? Most importantly—would people go out and buy it?

That was all still a little way off, though. For now, she had lots of clothes to try on, she'd had a chance to see people she knew, and she might even be able to catch up on her sleep again. For a little while. For the immediate moment, life looked pretty good to Brandy.

FIVE

It was September 1994 before the world was really introduced to Brandy, the singer. That was when the first single, "I Wanna Be Down," from the upcoming album (which would simply be entitled *Brandy*) was released. To support it, and also to make way for the album, she played a few shows around the country. Not just any shows, but really high-profile gigs, opening for megaacts like Boyz II Men and the woman she'd idolized for almost ten years, Whitney Houston. It was enough to make her starstruck, or it would have been if they weren't all so supportive and down-to-earth with her.

Sonja went on the road with her daughter, to make sure she was taken care of and also act as chaperone. It was a major start to her career, and a sure sign that Atlantic was going to push her record. There was already a video for "I Wanna Be Down," which had cost literally thousands of dollars to make. No sooner was it out than the song was all over urban radio, with the Top Forty stations soon following. It seemed impossible to believe at first, but week by week Brandy could follow its progress up the charts, top forty, then twenty, then ten. On the R&B charts it went all the way to Number One—a totally amazing debut.

Of course, there was more to it all than jetting around and playing major shows. There were all kinds of promotional chores to be done, the daily tutoring, traveling from one city to another and a permanent feeling of jet-lag and homesickness. And always the stage fright gripping her before she had to get out and perform, even though she seemed to have the audience in the palm of her hand from the moment she appeared onstage.

And when she was at home, her new success and routine let her know who her real friends were. Some, as she quickly realized, had gone because "they get jealous." And there were new people, who liked her because she was Brandy, the successful singer, not because of who she really was.

Every day saw three hours of tutoring, no matter what else was happening, and a couple of hours of vocal training. Her voice was her instrument, and she had to keep it in perfect shape. It all meant that her life was very far from normal. But that was fine.

"I knew I had to make a sacrifice to do what I've always wanted to do," she said.

One of the promotions that involved Brandy was on *The Box*'s "94 Days of Summer."

"It's a weeklong contest that culminates in a grand-prize winner escorting Brandy as she visits each of the seven Six Flags amusement parks across the country," explained Richard Nash, the senior vice president of black music at Atlantic.

Inevitably, because of her age, Brandy was going to be compared to another new teen singer, Aaliyah, whose album, *Age Ain't Nothing But A Number*, had done so well. Aaliyah, who, at fifteen, was the same age as Brandy, had exploded with two big R&B singles, "At Your Best (You Are Love)" and "Back and Forth," which, combined with her album, had really put her in the spotlight, and made her the teen standard. But there were definite differences between them, as Nash pointed out.

"Aaliyah has more of a street edge, and image-wise she's harder. Brandy is a little more refined, with a sportier look." In other words, she was much more the typical teen, which was no bad thing; it helped more people relate to her. That was definitely true at the end of 1994, when it was revealed that Aaliyah, still not sixteen, had married producer and singer R. Kelly—nothing like that was on the horizon for Brandy.

And for the first time she was willing to come out and talk about her involvement in various community causes. She wasn't there just because it was what people in the entertainment industry did, but because that sense of responsibility to others was something that had been drummed into her from birth. It came with the territory when you were an active member of your church, which Brandy had always been, and would always continue to be.

"I'm an ambassador for the Sabriya House," she explained, "and visit ill children in the hospital. I also help out with the Brotherhood Crusade. I may be young, but I can already see that you only get out of life what you put in, and music and TV aren't everything."

With a lot of artists, particularly ones who'd worked a long time and were just starting to enjoy success, that might have seemed like lip service, but in Brandy's case it happened to be genuine. To most people she'd happened overnight, first with *Thea* and now a big single. But she'd worked long and hard for this moment, and only hoped she could sustain it in November when *Brandy* finally appeared.

She needn't have worried. By the beginning of 1995, *Brandy* had already been certified gold, meaning it had sold more than half a million copies, and by her birthday she had her first platinum disc, with more than one million copies bought. It was something she'd always dreamed about, as far back as she could remember, but nothing compared with the reality. Even if *Entertainment Weekly* dismissed it as "a premature effort, at best," offering the record a "C," it struck a chord with the people who really mattered—the ones who were willing to go to the store and spend their hard-earned cash.

A lot of time and effort had gone into creating *Brandy*. It came from her heart.

"Music is in me," she said. "I sing about the truth and what I believe in."

While it didn't have the same street edge as Aaliyah, that was cool; Brandy had never pretended to know the street. She was a middle-class girl whose main entertainment was the mall. She might sing about romance, but in real life she'd never had a boyfriend—according to her parents, she was too young to date, and anyway, where was she going to find the time for any kind of love thang?

The sales of *Brandy* made it obvious that this wasn't going to be something that was just flavor of the month. Even after the million mark, it just kept climbing and climbing, and the second single, "Baby" did every bit as well as the first, backed by a video directed by Hype Williams, who'd also shot the video for the remix of "I Wanna Be Down," which featured some big female names from hip-hop—MC Lyte, Queen Latifah, and Yo Yo.

Everyone wanted Brandy. *MTV News* had interviews, radio stations wanted her live on the air, she appeared on *The Tonight Show* with Jay Leno. It was amazing. The world seemed to be exploding around her. People wanted to work with her. She made a video with Boyz II Men, and then Lenny Kravitz, the retro-rocker who'd been married to Lisa Bonet from *The Cosby Show*, and had become an international music star, asked her to work with him on a song for the *Batman Forever* soundtrack, "Where Are You Now."

One of the bonuses of that job was that she was given an invitation to attend the premiere of *Batman Forever*, where she was seated next to Will Smith. He wasn't a mega-movie star yet, but he'd topped the charts as a rapper and had five seasons of the hit sitcom, *The Fresh Prince of Bel Air*. Every time her song appeared he'd yell "Go Brandy! Go Brandy!" so loudly that people would turn and stare, totally embarrassing her—but in a good way.

What she really hoped was that "Where Are You Now" would be a single off the soundtrack (it wasn't), because "I really want to meet Chris O'Donnell. And I know if that's the single, then he's gonna probably be in the video."

She might be an established star now, but it didn't stop her gushing over someone else.

By the middle of 1995, some eight months after its release, *Brandy* was still in the charts, and had gone platinum four times—selling a staggering total of four million copies! It was far more than anyone could have expected, even the record company. For Brandy herself, it was as if she'd be catapulted to Wonderland. Everything was unreal. She was still playing gigs, putting it on for the people all over America.

And people were obviously still taking notice. She got a call from *Seventeen* magazine, who, along with Sears, were starting a program called Peak Performance. It was meant to be partly inspirational for teenage girls, but also something that would offer girls scholarships for college. What they wanted was for Brandy to be the first spokesperson for the program, and they were asking because not only was she a teen who'd made it herself, a widely recognized figure, but also because, in her studies, Brandy was a straight-A student.

How could she refuse?

It meant she'd be even busier, going to malls around the country to speak to audiences of girls. It would certainly put her in closer proximity to her fans than she'd been since she'd become a star. There'd be autographs to sign, a couple of songs to sing to a backing tape, and most importantly, information to tell the girls about the Peak Performance program, to encourage them to do the very best they could. At least it would give her some time in her schedule to actually go to malls and do a little shopping as well!

It was an honor to be asked, but one that Brandy had more than earned. Already she was thinking ahead, with plenty of encouragement from Sonja and Willie, to college. A high school diploma was fine, it was a start, but there was no substitute for a college degree in the modern world. She wanted to make her living from singing and from acting, but who could tell what might lie in the future?

In the way of showing what a small world it really was, the following year the Peak Performance spokesperson would be Jennifer Love Hewitt, with whom Brandy would work in 1998 on *I Still Know What You Did Last Summer*.

In a very short time Brandy had gone from being an unknown singer who'd had a part on a failed TV sitcom to a teen icon, a role model for girls. Could she be as sweet as she seemed? Could anyone be that nice, that charming, and that modest when they'd had three hit singles and a hit album?

The answer, of course, was yes. She certainly didn't have any kind of wild streak. But at the same time, she didn't even try and pretend that she was perfect.

"I'm really not," she said. "I make mistakes, and I'm human. But I'm not wild." Really, she was just like anybody else.

"I'm not the perfect angel. I have pain just like everybody else. I have people that I like. I have people that I don't like. I'm a regular human being."

And, like any other teen, there were times she'd clash with her parents. It was inevitable in any family situation, but even more so when you mother was also your manager. Once she'd even made Sonja cry.

"Sometimes I can be disrespectful and talk back," she explained. "I told her, 'Mommy, sometimes you work too much. You stay in the office too much and sometimes I feel like my mother is not here. Sometimes I want to talk to you as a mother, not as a manager.' And she took it all wrong. She kind of felt like I was saying she wasn't a good mother, but that's not what I was saying. So I had to make it up to her."

But those were the ups and downs of adolescence. And if that was as bad as it became, the Norwoods, as a family, had gotten off very lightly.

Even younger brother Ray J. wasn't any kind of a handful. By now he'd signed his own record deal with Atlantic, and was slowly being groomed toward his first album.

The concentration, though, had to be on Brandy. She was the one who was on fire. In some ways it left Sonja caught in the middle, trying to juggle the roles of mother and manager. In both cases she had to be very protective of her little girl, but she also had to strike a balance between the two. Overall, she managed it well. According to Brandy, there weren't "many mothers like [Sonja] in this industry. She says what she wants and isn't going to let anybody get over on me. She's strong, but she lets me have my freedom. She's a good mother, and I love her."

The spats they had were just that—spats. The Norwoods had always been a very close family, devoted to each other and to their faith, and no amount of success was going to change that.

At sixteen, it seemed as if Brandy had it all. Three hit singles, a massive album that continued to do great business. She'd toured with the best, been asked to perform with other great names, been on the soundtrack of a huge film. Everything was going her way. America knew her name. She was a new R&B diva. And she'd kept her feet firmly planted on the ground through it all.

She continued, in a quiet way, her community work. If anything, she was doing more of it than ever before, as people approached Sonja. One of the most important things was spending four weeks during the year touring high schools, telling other teens the absolute importance of staying in school and getting a diploma. It was done under the banner of BET (Black Entertainment Television), who had a Back to School program, aimed at those who'd dropped out, and to stop others from doing the same. Then there was the Earth Jam program, which also took her to high schools, giving demonstrations on recycling and protecting the environment.

Brandy took her position as a role model very seriously. For a long time she'd been involved with the Brotherhood Crusade and the Sabriya Castle. Now she was also part of the National Council of Negro Women, the Black Family Reunion, RAINN (Rape, Abuse, Incest National Network), and the music industry's Urban Aid/LIFEBeat organization, which persuaded her to take part in an all-star concert at New York's Madison Square Garden.

In many ways, a single album had made her into an important national figure. She didn't trumpet her involvement with all these different causes—she just helped out. It was part of life, part of being a citizen of earth.

Six

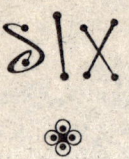

One album, and it had done so much for her.

Brandy might have had the voice of an adult, but a glance at the cover made it clear that the record company was marketing her as a teenager. With her braids in bunches, peeking out from under a cap, she looked thirteen or fourteen. Even the pictures inside the jacket showed someone who definitely looked young, her hair parted at the side, her face not yet the lovely chiseled thing it would become. Her bare midriff was covered by a backpack (as late as 1998, Sonja Norwood refused to allow a belly button shot of her daughter; that would have to wait for her first film), and she looked her age. Even the more sophisticated black-and-white shot showed a girl, not a woman. But that was all fine. Brandy didn't have to pretend she was older than she really was. The real surprise was if you heard her before seeing her, since she sounded about twenty years old, with a voice that could twist and turn around phrases quite knowingly and sensually, able to convey longing and wanting.

The emotions in the lyrics were as innocent as the

pictures, however. Romance looked up very often, but sex never reared its head. It was an album for teenage girls, and they all got it—big-time. It didn't try to be too hip, but to have a wide appeal. And for that, staying R&B was just fine. Hip-hop and R&B seemed to have pretty much taken over the charts. Considering that fifty years before R&B had been labeled "race music," America had moved on to embrace it in a massive way. The music had changed, and so had the audience, having crossed every racial boundary, which could only be a good thing, not merely for sales, but for unity. The bass was perfect for pounding in a car, for shaking up the neighborhood.

The fact that Brandy had a background singing in church colored her music, helped her put the emotion into it. Aretha had been a church singer, so had Marvin Gaye, so had so many great vocalists. She was part of a tradition. But the vocal training she'd received from her father also showed. Her voice could be silky smooth, as on the delicate, three-part, "I Dedicate," or a huskier growl. She could spring things around on a mid-tempo hit, a slow jam, a diva-ish ballad, or hit it with gospel fervor. What *Brandy* really proved, when it finally appeared toward the end of 1994, was that Brandy Norwood might have been a good actress on television, but as a singer she was an extraordinary talent.

It all opened up with "Movin' On," with a cool groove over a very funky bassline, and layers of backing vocals sliding in and out of the mix behind Brandy. She was in charge from note one. This was her song. The horns slid in here and there to offer some punctuation. Silky was what it was all about, held up by the bass and the drums, and on a very soulful tip, which was perfect, as Brandy's music was as much about soul as anything that had grown out of hip-hop. It anounced her intentions for the album. Nothing over the top, this record chilled, bringing in touches of jazz and letting her show her stuff. On this track, and throughout the album, it was the vocal arrangements that were the key. Lots of background vocals to carry the melody behind her, with the instruments sparse and down in the mix. Brandy contributed backgrounds to all the tracks, either alone, or helped by a small crew—Sheree Ford Payne, Rahsaan Patterson, Tiara Le Macks, Fuzzy, Tamara, Keishah Thomas, Robin Thicke, and Jeffrey Young. It was a style that worked, and highlighted Brandy's remarkable voice, bringing it front and center.

"Baby" was sultry without ever sinking down, very teenage and innocent, as Brandy really was herself, with some deep bass that just filled the body as it came out of the speakers. A love song, this wasn't about knockin' da boots, but getting to know someone, getting to trust and love them properly, and Brandy sounded totally convincing as someone in love, even though she'd never been in real life. It would be the second hit single off the record, and with its sneaky little hooks, it was an obvious winner, not only for R&B, but also Top Forty radio.

Then came "Best Friend." Brandy didn't write it, but she might as well have done, since the sentiments in the song were certainly hers. It was for Ray J., her little brother who was quickly growing up and making his own life.

"I can talk to him about everything and tell him

everything," she said. And in this she thanked him for being there for her, for being family and so close, the way brothers and sisters ought to be but all too often aren't. With the flute leading it slightly toward jazz, it was the kind of tune that would never be more than an album track, but that was fine. She got to shout out to her little bro, which was something she needed to do somewhere on here. There was more to this than Brandy doing it just for herself.

The big single that had broken Brandy all across the country was "I Wanna Be Down," and that was the next cut. It upped the tempo a little bit from the slow jam, getting decidedly in the pocket on the beat, perfect for playing in the Jeep, while Brandy went after the boy she really wanted in the lyrics, without every trying to get too overt. That innocence was perhaps a hard line to maintain, but the writers held to it well. Brandy could be cool and hip without ever getting into down and dirty territory. But R&B was more about romance and sex, the pure love of Boyz II Men rather than the blatant sexuality of The Artist Formerly Known As Prince.

Next up was "I Dedicate (Part I)," the first of three "I Dedicate" snippets that run through the album, all co-written by Brandy. In a way, they were the glue that held it all together, a constant reminder that this wasn't just about Brandy herself, but the people who'd loved and inspired her though her life. Part I was the only part with lyrics, a chance to give real props to everybody. Musically, that included Aretha—well, how could she ignore the Queen of Soul?—Stevie Wonder, and Whitney Houston, whom she referred to on the CD sleeve as "my mentor—my inspiration. I may not know you, but you have influenced my musical career in many ways. You are the epitome of a songstress and I hope one day to be just like you musically. You have a place in my heart forever." With just under ninety seconds she couldn't acknowledge everyone, but the main people got in there.

"Brokenhearted" moved on to a slinky tip, with a soft keyboard line introducing a slow jam where Brandy managed to sound remarkably like Mariah Carey—the whole song sounded as if it could have come off Carey's *Dreamlover* album, restrained, sad, and...brokenhearted. Her voice wove a powerful spell around the lyrics, working in that huskier lower register, while never forgetting the basic groove of the song.

After that it was on to "I'm Yours," one of the few real ballads on the album. But even though it was a ballad, that didn't mean Brandy was plunging into diva country. That simply wasn't her. She could sing, but she didn't have a range of five octaves she needed to show off. Instead, it was all about putting the song, and the emotions of the song, across, the love she felt for the boy involved, and how she wanted to be with him, not just now, but forever. In other words, it had flava.

Musically, "Sunny Day" was the most upbeat tune on the album, which totally belied its words. He was gone, she was left alone, so why did it matter if it was a lovely day; on her own, every day was gray inside. But it bounced along on its drum pattern and bassline, with layers of backing vocals coming in like fluffy clouds behind Brandy's lead voice. The chorus repeated and pushed the point home, but it was impossible to disguise the truly sunny mood of the music—it would have been a perfect summer single if "I Wanna Be Down" hadn't been released then instead.

"As Long As You're Here" was a great slow jam, about trying to save a relationship, trying to clear the air and sort things out, with Brandy not just rolling over, but stating what *she* wanted, too, with a sax line (actually sampled and played on keyboard) running continuously behind everything, holding it all together, and offering a relaxed, jazzy vibe to everything.

The jazzy vibe continued in "Always On My Mind," which had some very subtle chord changes, very sophisticated, and a lovely showcase for Brandy's vocal abilities. Once again it owed a debt to Mariah in the way Brandy wrapped herself around a line, trading off the lead and background vocals in a very complex vocal arrangement. As with almost everything else on the record, it was about love—in this case, being crazy about someone, crushing on them, and having them on her mind. Written, arranged, and produced by Kenneth Crouch, it was apparent that he knew his way perfectly around this kind of song.

"I Dedicate (Part II)" had few words—not too much more than the title—but that didn't matter. It took the listener back to part one, and the people who were important in Brandy's life, the people who'd put her where she was, able to make this album. At fifty-five seconds it was little more than a moment, leading into "Love Is On My Side," a full-on ballad that showed Brandy's debt to Whitney Houston. By the standards of the rest of the album, it leaned close to the middle of the road, the kind of song you could play to mom and dad, that they'd understand and appreciate—Whitney, after all, had gone quite MOR after the dancey beginning. Still Brandy didn't try to take the diva route, no sustained high notes, since she was obviously much happier singing in a lower register. But it was relatively a big production, only missing the full orchestral treatment to make it complete. Perhaps the biggest surprise was that Atlantic didn't try this as a single to broaden Brandy's appeal. Or perhaps they thought, after three R&B and pop hits and four million copies of the album sold, she didn't need to broaden her appeal much further.

"Give Me You" had gospel overtones, particularly in Brandy's singing over the introduction, and the piano playing behind the vocal, which could have came straight out of church. As much as anything was on the record, this was the rawest track on the album. Like Mariah going gospel (which she had a couple of times, early in her career), this was Brandy at her best vocally, given pretty free rein to demonstrate her power over the song. And the girl was in definite command. Of course it was about love. In this case, without ever stating it, the love was that of Jesus, but with that great down-to-earth feel of *real* gospel. It could have stood as a modern gospel classic, not out of place late in the evening or early on a Sunday morning before (or even during) church.

And it all ended with "I Dedicate (Part III)," a wash of sound on which to go out, and bring the listener back to earth after the sway of the last track. Brandy was grateful to people, and she didn't want anyone to ever forget the debt that she owed.

It was a big album. For someone who wasn't even fifteen when she recorded it, it was a huge step. All those hours of practice with her father, of doing small gigs and working her way up to *Showtime at the Apollo* had paid off handsomely. As an artistic achievement, it was great, something that helped capture her properly. *Brandy* didn't try and show Brandy Norwood as someone she wasn't. It didn't try and make her into a diva, didn't even try to make her more grown-up than she really was.

The fact that it was so well-received by people only indicated that Atlantic had done the right thing, every step of the way, with her. Four million copies of a debut album was a lot of product for a label, and it made Brandy a superstar in their book. The only downside to it all, if there was one, would be that even more would be expected the next time around. At least, the record business being what it was, that gave her another couple of years.

At one point, in the 1960s, artists had been expected to bring out two albums and four singles a year—a ridiculously large amount of material to have to write, record, and produce, considering that acts seemed to spend most of their time on the road, and the average recording session, to lay down *two* songs, lasted a total of three hours. Entire albums were recorded in a single day.

As acts sold more and more records, they had the luxury of being able to take more time, particularly once album sales became greater than singles. It became one album a year, then one album every two years—which was okay when the artist was going platinum. A few singles could be taken from each album and spaced out, to keep the sales alive. A longer sales cycle allowed the record companies to maximize the potential of each release.

That was the world Brandy came into. *Brandy* came out late in 1994, which meant that about a year later, under normal circumstances, she would have thought about going back into the studio. Sales of the album had peaked, she'd enjoyed three major hit singles, and it was time to think about doing it all over again. She'd spent time on the road, most particularly with Boyz II Men, who were still mega next to her. They'd been there and done that, more than once.

There was only one drawback. Brandy was in no rush to go ahead and make another record. It was as if she'd already done too much, too quickly in the music business, and she had no wish to burn out on it all, not if she was going to be around it for many years to come. She needed a friend to talk to, someone who understood, and she found one in the person of Boyz II Men singer, Wayna Morris.

SEVEN

"For so long I was his best friend," Brandy said about Wayna. "I was like his little sister."

The two of them talked every day on the phone, but there was no question of a relationship, at least not yet. Brandy was back home in Carson, but Boyz II Men were still out on the road, and they were going to be busy for months to come. Besides, Brandy was just sixteen, and her mother didn't want her dating yet.

"I don't think he liked me when I was a young girl. But I, like, grew up right in front of him. I grew up in his eyes."

She was growing up quickly, not only because of the days passing, but also because of the business she was in. That demanded a more adult, very professional attitude, and Brandy was definitely a professional.

"Show business is trying to take over my life," she admitted, "and the trick is to make sure it isn't my life." Still, she knew it was only temporary. "I make sure I do some normal things like going to the mall, shopping and hanging out with my friends. I'll fight to keep a lot of normality in my life, otherwise I could turn into some kind of obnoxious, big-headed monster."

Given her normal, sweet personality, that seemed highly unlikely, but it was good that she was aware of the possibility; that way it definitely wouldn't happen.

There was no doubt, however, that her life was moving at hyperspeed these days.

"It feels that way now because I have to do so much work with touring and recording, and I may even have a new CBS-TV series!"

Actually, the series had been brewing for a few months, more or less since her album had appeared in the stores.

The idea for *Moesha* had had its birth in 1993, when Sara Finney and Vida Spears, who'd worked together for years, came up with the idea for a very positive sitcom about an African-American family.

"The images out there of black families are so negative," Spears explained. "They're falling apart, there's somebody missing in the home. But most families are hard-working... they work to raise their families, they love their children, and they want to give them everything they can."

They began to pitch their idea to the different networks, but the big question was what young actress could carry the lead role?

At that point the duo asked Ralph Farquhar, who'd worked on *South Central*, to come on board with them. They focused their ideas, made the characters more real, and returned to CBS, explaining their concept. The network said they were "committed to putting a family show featuring African-Americans on the air," Farquhar recalled, and with that, a script was written, the lead being a fourteen-year old girl.

The big problem was the fact that they didn't have a fourteen-year old girl to star in the series. CBS told them, "Bring us a fourteen-year-old black girl star and you've got a show. So that was like saying 'Pass.' Then Vida and Sara mentioned Brandy to me."

If Brandy was interested, then the writers would have to re-work the script, making Moesha (it's pronounced Mo-EESH-a, as if you didn't already know) a little older. But that was the least of their problems. The two big questions were, would she be interested, and could she carry a show on her shoulders?

She already had a major hit single, and was gearing up for the release of *Brandy*. There was no doubt that Brandy Norwood was so hot she was sizzling. And would Sonja, as both her manager and her mother, want Brandy to focus on more than her music?

Secondly, her role in *Thea* hadn't been that large. This would be something altogether different. She'd be the lead, the focus of the show, and that would require a lot from her, in terms of energy, commitment, and ability. Would she be up to that job?

There was only one way to find out about it all, and that was to ask. Farquhar knew the Norwoods already. He'd been the executive producer of *The Sinbad Show*, where Willie, Jr. had made his debut. Farquhar called Willie, Sr., and was put in touch with Sonja, who asked to see the pilot script that had already been written.

A lot depended on her answer. Luckily, she loved it. Being part of a stable black family herself, it reflected her own life, and it offered a positive outlook. She showed the script to her daughter.

"At first I said, 'What kind of name is Moesha?'" Brandy recalled. "After I read the script I was like, 'This girl is me!'"

Brandy was in. She joined the *Moesha* team for a meeting with the suits at CBS, and a pilot was made. Brandy astonished everyone with the ease with which she seemed to handle the role. It was as if she'd been right—the girl really was her, and she was Moesha.

CBS loved the pilot. However, they had no place on their schedule for it.

"We ran up against, 'Well, we don't have anything to pair this with,' said Farquhar. "Essentially, most programmers think that if you have a black half-hour teenage family comedy, you need to have another one to pair it with."

At that point, ABC made an offer for the show, willing to put in straight into their schedule in the middle of the 1994-95 season. Although CBS wasn't about to start airing it, neither were they going to give it up to their opposition. Unable to wait, ABC gave up the chase.

There was more interest, though, from the brand-new UPN network. They'd seen the pilot and liked it, feeling it would work well for them. Even if they couldn't get it immediately, they seemed to figure that CBS would never find a place for it. If they were patient, then all good things would come to them. As it was, UPN only had one show with any kind of national impact in the ratings, *Star Trek: Voyager*. To get something that could be just as big was worth the wait.

On October 27, 1995, it all paid off. The option CBS

had on *Moesha* expired, and UPN, as good as their word, signed contracts for the show, initially for thirteen episodies.

"The opportunities that are presented to us as African-American writer/producers have come largely from the new networks," Farquhar said. "With these new networks, more diversity is appearing, and people such as ourselves are getting a serious shot."

Given the rigors of preparing a season, Spears and Finney, who were also writing for *The Parent'hood* on WB, brought six other writers on board the staff. The original concept of *Moesha* had called for the father, Frank, who was a widower, to be raising both his kids, Moesha and Myles, alone, to show, as Finney said, "black men who take care of children."

That changed, in large part, because of Farquhar's experience on *South Central*, where the family was headed by a single mother.

"There is the extra scrutiny that a black show is subjected to when it hits the airwaves nowadays, especially from the black audience. They're going to say, and the press is going to say, 'Is this stereotypical, are they shucking and jiving?' I think we've managed to avoid that."

They avoided it in every way, bringing in a stepmother who was a good woman, very far from the wicked stereotype. The adjustment she had to make to the family—and the family to her—brought in some interesting dynamics and opened up a lot of storyline possibilities.

The big thing for *Moesha* was Brandy. By the time the show had been given the go-ahead from UPN, she'd been a star for a year. Her album was multi-platinum. Among teens she was pretty much a household name. Getting her in the series was a serious coup, because it meant a lot of people—particularly young people, whom every network was courting—would tune in just to see her. At least, they would for the first episode. And it if went well, if the show was as good as everyone believed it to be, those people would return week after week. But the show at least began with a built-in audience, which was better than most new television ventures.

"It's a strange time in the land of TV, and a lot of forces conspired to allow us to be able to do this show," Farquhar mused. He pointed out that the "depiction of African-Americans, except on *Cosby*, hasn't been very good. One of the roles of TV is to educate. I think a show like this allows anyone to sit down and watch and feel comfortable."

Although the producers had assembled a strong ensemble cast, it all really hinged on whether Brandy was believable as Moesha. Farquhar certainly had faith in her abilities.

"She brings complete legitimacy to the part of a teenager," he said. "She's the real deal."

And she was totally enthusiastic about the project.

"I like it because it's fresh, it's now, it's new. It's not like a lot of TV shows you see because it's really real. [Other shows] don't say what kids are really like, really going through, and I think we do," Brandy said.

William Alan Young was cast as Frank Mitchell, a widower raising two kids alone, the nine-year-old fireball, Myles (Marcus T. Paulk), who was never short of a sassy remark, and fifteen-year-old Moesha (Brandy).

Frank, who made his living as a salesman of Saturn automobiles, and who loved his work, was something of an over-protective parent when it came to his daughter. He'd determined that she wouldn't date before she was sixteen, which didn't sit too well with a girl who was eager to spread her wings a little—without getting into too much trouble.

It was Moesha who bookended each episode, writing in her diary, letting the audience know how she felt about things, her family, her life, about the future. For three years, since her mother passed away, Moesha had been the woman of the house, with all manner of daily responsibilities that she took very seriously, and which had made her a little more adult than many of her classmates.

Into this equation walked Dee Mitchell (Sheryl Lee Ralph), Frank's new wife. Moesha was naturally resentful of someone new coming in and not only taking her mother's place, but also usurping the role she'd taken on in the family. It was enough for her to believe that Dee was the classic horrible stepmother, and that was the way she'd initially treat her.

But Dee was a teacher, and a good one, dedicated to her profession. She was used to dealing with kids, even kids of Moesha's age. She knew that Frank was cosseting his kids too much, and she knew that her role in the family was a particularly difficult one, that it would take time for the kids to acknowledge and accept her as a person, and as a mother. Never quite their mother, but a parent, nonetheless.

The show was set in the Leimert Park section of Los Angeles, where the Mitchells lived. It wasn't Bel Air, but neither was it the Watts of *Sanford and Son*. This was a middle-class family, with the kind of aspirations many families of any color could relate to. At the same time, it made no attempt to try and be a white family sitcom. The language of the teens was black slang, peppered with lots of black cultural references. That, the creators hoped, was part of its appeal. It didn't talk down to its audiences. If you knew what the words meant, what "whack" was, who Zora Neale Hurston was, and what her importance had been, fine. If not, you weren't going to get an explanation, and you probably didn't want one, because you wouldn't really be down with what was happening.

It aimed to have the hip-hop quality that *Fresh Prince of Bel Air* had tried for, and sometimes managed, mostly due to the presence of Will Smith. But it also aimed to be a family show, something parents and children could watch together, that would impart positive values and a feeling of togetherness. Trying to resolve those two things wasn't the easiest thing in the whole world, and it would demand a lot from the show's writers. They wouldn't be preachy or dorky. And most especially, they couldn't be precious about anything—teens certainly weren't. A small dose of cynicism was definitely in order.

And for Brandy, it was a huge chance to prove herself. After the failure of *Thea*, with which she hadn't been too pleased, this was the opportunity for millions of people each week to decide about her acting skills. She already had it made as a singer, that was beyond any doubt. But most people didn't even know that she *could* act. And could she portray a normal teenage girl. After all, for the last year her life had been anything but normal. Most teens didn't release multi-platinum albums and share the stage with Boyz II Men anywhere but in their dreams.

It also meant that her schedule was going to be horrendously crowded. A TV show translated into a *lot* of work, long hours five days a week (although, as Brandy was still only sixteen, she still couldn't legally work more than ten-and-a-half hours each day, with some of that given over to school, very important as she was now in her last year of high school, having been pushed ahead a grade, and was already looking forward to college). When she'd been on *Thea*, trying to juggle everything had been rough. Now, as the star of this show, it was going to be ten times worse. Everything, and everyone, depended on her being really good.

In many ways, the character of Moesha was an outlet for Brandy. It gave her the chance to be the normal teen she'd never had the opportunity to be in real life, to explore and experience that side of things, even if it was under the lights and in front of an audience. So it offered her a catharsis, a chance to see what she'd lost, and to be able to relate more to her friends, most of whom weren't in show business in any way.

At least fame hadn't gone to her head. She might travel by limo now, with a driver waiting for her, but she still liked to stop at the drive-thru window at McDonald's for her meals. So some part of her remained a normal teenager.

But could she make everyone else believe that?

* * *

Moesha's season began in January of 1996, and the first episode—which was actually the pilot that had been filmed a year before—focused on Moesha, while introducing the rest of the characters. She was having difficulty handing over the reins of the family to Dee, but at the same time, she was eager to spread her wings and be a teenager a little. The only problem was that her father wouldn't let her date yet, and there was a boy she liked, and who she thought liked her—Ohagi (Merlin Santana). However, when she turned up at a party and saw him kissing another girl she realized that all his poetic words hadn't meant much. She went home to find comfort in a place she'd never expected—from her new stepmother.

The next week, the head cheerleader asked Moesha to try out for the squad, something she decided she didn't really want to do. But Mo's best friend, Kim (Countess Vaughn), *really* wanted to be a cheerleader, so she could be the "next Paula Abdul," and she managed to persuade Moesha to come along and audition for moral support. The only problem was that Kim made the squad, and Moesha—who'd seemed like she would just walk in—didn't. All of a sudden Kim was running with a new crew, and Moesha was jealous enough to destory their friendship—almost. But not quite. At home, Frank was learning to cope with the fact that he'd married an older woman, after discovering that Dee was one whole year older than him, while their neighbor, Hakeem (Lamont Bentley) was eating everything in sight, trying to gain weight in an attempt to make the basketball team.

For Brandy, this show held a few special memories,

since it gave her one of those opportunities to be a normal teen.

"I tried out to be a cheerleader, and it hit me that this was the only way I'd ever get the chance to," she said.

The following episode saw Moesha turn sixteen (coincidentally, the same week that Brandy actually turned seventeen). There was a party, but far more importantly, Brandy could now date. She waited for all the offers to come from boys, but there was a resounding silence, which did her self-confidence no good at all, until Hakeem took her aside and pointed out that the reason no one was asking her out was that they were intimidated by both her and her father. Frank, meanwhile, was going through the usual parental agonies as his daughter moved toward dating. Finally, Moesha received an invitation for an "unoffical" date from Ohagi, the boy who broke her heart not long before, and she accepted. Before she could go, however, it wasn't Frank who sat her down for a talk about sex, but Dee, making the bond between them a little tighter.

Interestingly, at the fictional birthday party, male guests were frisked for guns, a sign of reality intruding into the dreamworld of the program, but one defended by Ralph Farquahr.

"The studio questioned why it was called for," he explained. "But during these times you have to take precautions. These are realities the show takes seriously."

The following week saw Moesha, normally very tight with her money, lending Hakeem twenty dollars. However, the repayment he'd promised didn't seem to be forthcoming, and he was nowhere to be found. After a couple of weeks Moesha decided to track him down.

Cornering him, he admitted, ashamed and embarrassed, that his mother had been laid off from her job, and he didn't have the money. A job for Hakeem seemed like the perfect solution, so Moesha and the rest of her family encouraged him to apply for one at the mall, selling athletic shoes—after all, he was a basketball nut. Moesha even went so far as to lend him one of her father's suits—the costly Armani that Dee had given Frank. But in the end, it all came to nothing, as Hakeem blew the interview; hard work wasn't his interest, just money.

In "Million Boy March" it was girls against boys at school. Moesha and Kim wanted to join the Council of Concerned Youth, who supposedly wanted to do things to improve the community and help teens who were at risk. Until they applied, however, the group had been all-male, led by the very sexist senior, Whitlock Green (Chaz Lamar Shepherd), whose mind seemed to be in the nineteenth century, when a woman's place was in the kitchen. Moesha wasn't about to stand for that. She had ideas and an organizational flair, and she wasn't shy about opening her mouth. The main thing the group needed was money, so she put together a fundraiser that was bound to be a success, since it starred R&B band Jodeci. When he saw what Moesha could do, Green had no alternative but to eat his words, and let her and Kim into the group—as well as perform some serious rethinking of his beliefs.

This episode was a family affair in more ways than one, since, guesting in the role of Charles was none other than Brandy's little brother, Willie, Jr., going under his stage name of Ray J.

Frank had been thinking of ways to surprise his

sixteen-year-old daughter, and the best surprise he could think of was something every teen wanted—a brand-new car. The problem was that what he thought was acceptable and what Moesha wanted were not too close. He was thinking about a Saturn (after all, he sold them, loved his work, and believed in them). Her heart was set on a Jeep; after all, that was what the really cool people drove, and it would definitely get her noticed at school. So when Frank presented her with the keys to her very own Saturn, she was less than overwhelmed. In fact, she didn't want it. For her, it was a Jeep or nothing. Not only did she hurt her father's feelings, standing on principle meant that Frank might easily take the gift away again. It was all up to Moesha. Did she want to live in a dream world, or accept reality, and have a new car? Reality, of course, won.

Moesha had done well in the ratings from the first week it aired. Everyone had expected strong initial reaction, mostly because of Brandy's presence, but as the season progressed, viewing figures stayed high—high enough to make it UPN's top sitcom. Not only that, but the reviewers liked it. In *People*, the review declared that "in its substance, look (fly fashions) and sound, this could be a real trendsetter." *Entertainment Weekly* declared it "smart, fast, and confident, *Moesha* sets a new standard for kid-friendly family entertainment." So it would come as no big surprise when it ended up beating out more than one hundred other shows to win a 1996 Parents' Choice Award, because, according to a spokesperson, "Brandy is so level-headed. The show's got backbone."

But it could also be silly, as "Chain, Chain, Chain"

proved. It revolved around a chain letter that everyone seemed to receive. Moesha, no believer in superstition, burned hers, and convinced Hakeem and her father to do exactly the same with theirs. Things, of course, began to go bad, not only in the family, but also at The Den, where all the teens hung out, and which had been preparing a big event—owner Andell (Yvette Wilson, who'd been in *Thea* with Brandy) had lost her chain letter. Andell's solution was to bring in a healer to cleanse The Den of evil spirits, and it seemed to work. It gave Moesha an idea, and at home she became a healer herself, trying to put her suddenly-arguing family back on the right track. It was pure fluff, but it was entertaining fluff.

Next week saw the show itself back on track, as Moesha dealt with the issue of responsibility. She'd long wanted to be earning money of her own, and the chance came when she and Kim won jobs in "market research" (actually consumer surveys) at the mall. It was very part-time, and quite manageable. Mo, of course, was good at her job, and was soon offered a promotion, which she accepted. Neither Frank nor Dee was too happy at that, since it meant more hours at work, and less applying herself to schoolwork. But Moesha wanted to be treated like an adult. They decided to let her accept the position, if only to let her see that being an adult wasn't all she thought it would be. Grown-up was more a state of mind than an age, and it meant a lot less of something that Moesha valued—her free time. And, of course, they were right. Mo was soon chafing at having no time to do the things she wanted to do. A lesson was learned quite quickly.

Moesha had slowly been accepting Dee as a part of the family, but it was taking time, and there will still a great deal she was holding back, not too surprisingly. Dee understood that all too well, as a teacher and as an adult. Things took a turn for the better when Dee's teenage neice, Charisse (Kellie Williams), came to visit the Mitchells, and Moesha saw a side of her stepmother that she'd never let herself see before—that Dee could could funny, charming, and down. The result was that Mo began looking at Dee with new eyes, and liking her more—possibly even loving her. Certainly the bond between the two of them deepened during and after the visit. Meanwhile, Andell was excited. She had a date with an old boyfriend. Not just any old boyfriend, but someone who'd gone on to make quite a name for himself—Deion Sanders, the guy who seemed to play every sport known to man. To be fair, it was an excuse to bring in a big name to boost the ratings for a week, but it worked, and Deion *did* lend an extra, and extra-large, dimension to the show.

"Reunion" tackled the very sensitive issue of interracial dating. While it shouldn't be an issue at all, the fact remains that it is, and someone needed to address it. In this case, it came about because Frank organized a reunion of the play group Moesha had been part of when she was an infant. The kids were all sixteen now (and, coincidentally, all Saturn owners). What Frank hadn't anticipated was romantic sparks between Mo and the boy who'd been her best friend back then, Matt (Andrew Keegan). The problem was that Matt was white. They wanted to date, but Frank was opposed. Not out of any racism, but out of a concern for his daughter. Nor was he the only one opposed. In the end the couple bowed to outside pressure.

It was, perhaps, the most important episode of the season, largely for the social issues it did raise. It forced viewers to think, and consider their own prejudices, which could only be a good thing. The underlying moral was that people should be taken for who they are, not their background or the color of their skins.

But it was a season for lessons, really, and Moesha got one in the next episode. She was competing against her classmate Gabriella (Samantha Becker, from *Saved By The Bell: The New Class*) for a prestigious internship with the *L.A. Times*. It would all depended on the stories they wrote. Thanks to Hakeem, Gabriella got the head start with a great piece. Now the pressure was on Moesha to come up with something better. And she did, in the form of an article about the ditch parties being thrown by her friends. However, the school's vice-principal somehow managed to get hold of a copy of the piece, and Mo was in big trouble. He wanted names, and if he didn't get them Mo would be suspended. If she did betray her friends, then the article could be considered for her internship . . . it was a tough choice she had to make, but she ended up doing what she believed was the right thing.

The following week offered a poignant take on Mother's Day. It began with Mo having all her money stolen from her locker, money she'd been planning to use to buy a Mother's Day present. Frank came to the rescue with cash, since he wanted this to be a special occasion for Dee. He'd planned a family brunch. But Mother's Day brought back memories of Moesha's natural mother, and all the grief she still felt at her loss. She couldn't go to something honoring Dee as her mother—and she didn't. When she failed to show, Frank knew where he'd find her, and went looking. Mo was at her mother's grave, remembering, and grieving, visited by a gospel group (played by Out of Eden), who performed "Lovely Day." It was tough, and there were no easy answers. Frank certainly didn't want her to forget her mother. At the same time he knew that life had to move on, and Mo had to accept Dee. But it was going to take time. . . .

Frank and Dee wanted to cement their marriage with a child of their own, before it became too late for them both. Myles liked the idea of a baby brother or sister, until Mo—who was absolutely against it—convinced him that a new baby would mean he'd receive a lot less attention, and that he'd end up babysitting and changing diapers all the time. Even then, Myles wasn't sure he believed her, until Frank, his "attention" more on Dee, forgot some plans he'd made with his son. Distraught, Myles ran away, which set everyone—family, neighbors, and friends—frantically searching for him, and Moesha realizing she'd taken things too far.

The season ended with romance—but not for Moesha. Instead, it was Hakeem who found a girlfriend, and Mo realized she actually missed him bugging her all the time. Kim missed him, too, but for different reasons—she didn't like the idea of Hakeem dating anyone but her. So Kim devised a scheme to break up the couple, and Mo agreed to help her. As soon as they'd succeeded, though, Moesha just felt guilty, and decided to do everything she could to patch things up again. She should have felt happy for Hakeem, instead of being so selfish. Meanwhile, Dee was doing a little matchmaking of her own, trying to pair Andell off with J.W. (Ricky Harris), one of Frank's colleagues from the Saturn dealership. Moesha had grown up a little, learned more about herself, and about the world, and her place in it—and about the nature and delicacy of relationships.

It was a good way to end a season that had been nothing short of triumphant. UPN's faith in the idea of *Moesha*, and of Brandy Norwood as the title character, had been amply rewarded. The viewing figures were strong, and had remained strong all season, from the time the show first appeared in January.

The revelation had been Brandy. She'd fitted into her role as comfortably as if it had been made for her—which it had, in many ways. The girl could really act. Add that to her singing, and it seemed like there was nothing she couldn't do.

And CD buyers weren't the only ones recognizing how great that voice of hers sounded. At the beginning of 1996, she found herself nominated for a Grammy, as Best Newcomer (which she didn't win), and also for Best Soul/R&B New Artist at the American Music Awards—which she definitely and justifiably *did* win—and where she also performed for a large television audience. Not going home with a Grammy was a disappointment, but at the *Soul Train* awards, a little over a month later, she made up for it by winning R&B New Artist for "I Wanna Be Down."

But far more than any awards, Brandy made a splash in the news during the spring when she joined Kobe Bryant as his prom date for his senior prom at Lower

Kickin' it at the Nickelodeon Kids' Choice Awards.
(NEAL PRESTON/RETNA)

At the MTV Video Awards, 1995. (BILL DAVILA/RETNA)

Brandy with her parents, Sonja and Willie Norwood. (GREG PACE/RETNA)

With her "fairy godmother," Whitney Houston. (JOHN SPELLMAN/RETNA)

Hangin' with little brother Ray J. (GREG PACE/RETNA)

With her vocal coach, a.k.a. Dad. (GREG PACE/RETNA)

Brandy and Whoopi Goldberg at the premiere of *Cinderella*. (ROB SIMMS/RETNA)

Hitting the runway for Candies. (ERNIE PANICCIOLI/RETNA)

Merion High School, just outside Philadelphia.

Bryant had become a very big deal by being the first basketball player to short-circuit college and enter the NBA draft directly from high school. People believed he was good enough to make it without those additional four years of coaching and polishing, and there was certainly plenty of interest. In the end, he'd show he was right, by joining the L.A. Lakers, and over a couple of years establishing himself as a star player.

He and Brandy had met at an awards show. They were both seniors now, both in the spotlight, and unable to have a completely normal life. Brandy, being tutored on the set, hadn't attended a regular school for a few years, so when he asked her to be his date, the offer was very tempting.

"When I met him I was like, 'Oh my God, you're cute,' " Brandy admitted. "The prom was so much fun. But we had talked every day before the prom so we could get to know each other. I was like, 'I'm not going to a prom with some guy I don't know.' He just seemed like a really, really nice person. So I asked my mom, and his mom talked with my mom."

Of course, immediately rumors began to circulate about a romance between the couple, but that was never the case. As she put it, "I was out with Kobe, chillin'. Just doing normal teenage stuff."

Bryant was important enough by himself to warrant national coverage of his high school prom. When it was learned that Brandy would be his date, the reporters and photographers seemed to gather in a pack. That made it rough for the other kids. They wanted to go and enjoy themselves—as did Kobe and Brandy—without a whole extra security crew.

But that was the price they had to pay, and it was mostly because of Brandy, who was already a star.

"It's not her fault," said one attendee, but noted, "We should be able to have our prom in peace."

Unfortunately, that was the cost of being Brandy, almost everywhere she went. She was popular. Every move was newsworthy, so every move had to be considered.

With *Moesha* on break for the summer, Brandy should really have begun recording her second album. But she didn't.

"She was really afraid," Sonja Norwood said. "She told us she never wanted to record a second album. So we gave her time to think it over."

As Brandy herself explained in the booklet that accompanied *Never Say Never*, "From 1996 to 1997, something happened—I didn't know until it was time to record that I was afraid to sing (sophomore jitters). I was comfortable just acting so it became difficult to go in the studio and really produce."

Excuses were made, anything to hold back the idea of going into a recording studio and beginning work on such a daunting project. After all, *Brandy* had been so huge. How could she ever hope to top that and fulfill everyone's expectations? It was a big weight to carry on the shoulders of someone who was still only seventeen. And that weight was made much heavier by the fact that she was the star of a hit television show. The pressure on her to excel at everything was tremendous, and something had to give. For now, it was the idea of recording.

The people who worked with her at Atlantic were understanding. Of course, they wanted another Brandy album out there, one that was bound to do very well, given her recent fame. But at the same time, they knew they'd end up with a much better record if they waited, and hoped the Brandy came to it in her own time.

For now, there was enough going on in her life. Nineteen ninety-six was the year she graduated from high school, which, without a ceremony, proved not to be the milestone she'd hoped it would be. But, at her parents' insistence, she did enroll in college, at Pepperdine in Malibu, where she'd begin studying psychology in the fall. Hardly a standard state university, but then she was a special case, someone who was working very full days, five days a week, and whose education could, at best, only be very part-time.

Her friendship with Wayna Morris continued to deepen. They talked often, getting to know each other better. She was busy rehearsing or taping. He was on the road with Boyz II Men or busy in the studio on some project or another. Their lives were chaotic, but it was a chaos they shared and could understand about each other. For the moment it remained platonic—in spite of all the rumors, Brandy wasn't dating *anyone*, and wouldn't until her eighteenth birthday—but it was beginning to edge away from that. At least, if and when a romance happened between the two of them, they'd already know each other well.

During 1995, Brandy had received a phone call she's never expected. From the time she'd really paid close attention to what was happening in music, Whitney

Houston had been her idol. The woman was a hitmaker, a true diva, she'd become a movie star, an all-around success. She was everything Brandy aspired to be. Even when Whitney had moved more toward the middle of the road in her music, Brandy had remained a committed fan. She had the kind of voice to die for, a great range and breath control (she held a note in the chorus of "I Will Always Love You" for what seemed like a superhuman amount of time). For technical ability, she was one of the very best around. Brandy had always been lavish and vocal in her praise of her heroine, even crediting her on "I Dedicate (Part I)" on *Brandy*. She saw Whitney as a mentor, someone who was up there while Brandy was still down here, a complete beginner in comparison.

So one thing she never expected was for Whitney to be calling *her*. That kind of thing just didn't happen. Even though Brandy was a star herself these days in the eyes of the public, that didn't stop her being a starstruck teenager.

Once she got over her astonishment, and found her voice enough to actually speak to this woman she'd thought of every day since she was seven, Brandy got to learn just why Whitney was calling. She was familiar with everything Brandy had said about her, had heard her album, and wanted to thank her. More than that, she was involved in a movie project, her first since *The Bodyguard*, three years before. It was a version of Terry McMillan's acclaimed novel, *Waiting to Exhale*. Babyface, the performer, producer of Toni Braxton and so many others, and owner of LaFace Records, was in charge of the music. And Whitney believed that Brandy should have a song on the soundtrack. She'd recommended her to Babyface, who was co-ordinating everything.

All this had happened right as *Moesha* began production in 1995, and Brandy was already swept off her feet by all the activity around her. There was no way she could make a decision without the approval of manager and mother, Sonja, but the chance to work on something as prestigious as this, to be associated with it in any shape or form, was thrilling. *Waiting to Exhale* had received so much praise as a book, an intimate and very honest look at the lives of some friends, the female side of the black experience. It was compassionate, funny, and gritty, all at the same time, a marvelous novel that had seemed almost like required reading, a book that almost mirrored the lives of many of its readers.

It was exactly the kind of thing that Sonja wanted Brandy to be associated with. Class was written all over it. Whitney herself would be on the soundtrack, although originally she'd had no plans to be.

Babyface had been recruited by the film's director, Forest Whitaker, while he was on tour with Boyz II Men.

"Forest met me backstage and surprised me by asking me to consider doing the score as well as the soundtrack," explained Babyface, also known as Kenny Edmonds. At that point, Whitney was simply going to star in the film, taking on the role of Savannah Jackson, until she heard a song she liked. In the end, Whitney recorded three—"Exhale (Shoop Shoop)," which went to Number One on the *Billboard* charts (giving Whitney her eleventh Number One hit), "Count on Me," which she co-wrote with Babyface, and sang as a duet with gospel star CeCe Winans, and "Why Does It Hurt So Bad," a song Babyface had written for her two years before, but which Whitney had never recorded.

She was very involved in the entire soundtrack process. Most soundtracks consisted of a variety of artists, seemingly randomly thrown together, often using songs the artists had already released elsewhere. *Waiting to Exhale* would be different.

"It was something Whitney and I talked about," said Babyface, "but I always thought it should be [all] females. So it was a question of Whitney helping me to pick her favorite singers and people she would want to be involved on the project."

That became a virtual who's-who of three generations of R&B singers. Aretha Franklin, the Queen of Soul, spoke for the sixties. The seventies were represented by names like Chaka Khan and Patti LaBelle, while the nineties offered Mary J. Blige, Toni Braxton, TLC, Sonja Marie, SWV, Chante Moore, Faith Evans, For Real, Shanna, and Brandy herself, with Whitney spanning the eighties and nineties.

Both soundtrack and film appeared at the end of November, 1995. The movie did tremendous business to match its ecstatic reviews. Having cost $15 million to make, it grossed over $66 million in the U.S. alone. On the back of that popularity, and the names of the people involved in its music, the album *Waiting to Exhale* was an immediate hit.

Whitney's single, "Exhale (Shoop Shoop)," which could almost have been a synopsis of the film's philosophy, was an automatic smash, too, entering the charts in the Number One position, where it stayed for a week, before being deposed by "One Sweet Day," the record-breaking hit by Mariah Carey and Boyz II Men.

It would prove to be one of the most successful soundtrack albums of the decade. With one exception (a version of "My Funny Valentine") every song was written or co-written by Babyface, who also handled all the production tasks. By March of 1996, when "One Sweet Day" finally ended its sixteen-week run at the top of the singles chart (giving way to Celine Dion and "Because You Loved Me," another soundtrack song, this time from *Up Close and Personal*, the Robert Redford/Michelle Pfeiffer vehicle), *two* songs from *Waiting to Exhale* were in the top five.

Mary J. Blige's "Not Gon' Cry" was at number four, and "Sittin' Up in My Room," Brandy's contribution, was one place higher. Neither would make the top position (Dion stayed Number One for six weeks, to be replaced by Mariah Carey solo), but that didn't lessen the impact of the songs, particularly "Sittin' Up in My Room," which became a staple both on MTV and on all manner of radio formats, eventually going platinum—and to sell a million copies of a *single* was no mean feat. A few months later, Toni Braxton's contribution to the soundtrack, "Let It Flow," which was the B-side of her "You're Makin' Me High" single, would also hit Number One for a week.

For Brandy, it was the perfect cap to complement the outfit of her album. *Brandy* and its singles had done so well. Now she'd shown she could be successful in another musical context, and as *Moesha* took off, it kept her name alive in the charts—and helped stave off the necessity of starting to think about a second album for a few more months.

She was grateful to Whitney, the woman she saw as her mentor, and to Babyface, for considering her for the project. There was a satisfaction about being associated with something like *Waiting to Exhale* that even her own album didn't bring. She'd been *asked*. And it would bring her something else, later in 1996—a nomination for Best Song at the MTV Movie Awards, alongside Whitney's "Exhale (Shoop Shoop)." To everyone's surprise, and pleasure, it wasn't Whitney who had to climb onto the stage to accept the award, but Brandy, who added this one to the collection she'd started earlier in the year. Never in a million years had she expected to outdo Whitney, but the older woman was more than gracious—she was totally glad for Brandy.

"Sittin' Up In My Room" had all the hallmarks of a Babyface production—a percolating popped bassline that propelled the song, gliding keyboards and funky little guitar lines. Brandy's voice was low over the verses, most definitely her, not sounding like Whitney or Mariah or anyone else. Then it all came to the chorus with slickly layered vocals that melted like butter. And in the chorus was the magic. It stuck to the brain as if it was covered in Velcro. There was no way the sound couldn't have been a hit. And Babyface knew it, as did Brandy. The song was a gift, and its style connected R&B past and present for anyone listening. Brandy gave it her all, sounding even more mature than she had on her own album, shining in some fine company. Using the chorus as a long fade was inspired, just to make absolutely sure it sank into people's minds and stayed there. And it paid off very, very well.

It had been a great year so far. Short of actually starting work on her new album, how could it have gone better for Brandy? But, just like school years, her calendar didn't run from January to December. Late July was the start of a new year for her, when cast and crew assembled for the second season of *Moesha*.

EIGHT

There had never been much doubt that *Moesha* would be renewed. It was the highest-rated sitcom on UPN, one of the few shows they carried that was even really registering in the Nielsen ratings. More than that, it was exactly the kind of show every network wanted—sensitive, compassionate, with strong family values, yet still totally hip, appealing to the young demographic that had advertisers drooling.

Having begun in January, the first season had only really been half a season. This time out the first show would be broadcast August 27, 1996, and run until May of 1997.

By now everyone had bonded. They'd become a substitute family for each other. William Allen Young, who played Frank Mitchell, said that "Brandy represents the daughter I wish I had. She's intelligent. She's outgoing. She stands on her own two feet and she tells you the truth."

He saw Brandy Norwood, the person, as opposed to Brandy, the star. If there was any friction on the set, it was between Brandy and Countess Vaughn, who played her best friend, Kim Parker. The two weren't exactly close friends, although they still managed to work well together.

"Countess told me that she was the reason the show was so successful," Brandy recounted, "and then she called me out of my name, she called me a bitch, and I didn't like that at all." Brandy's response was to tell her, "I don't want to be disrespected any longer in front of everyone. Please excuse me."

It was a mature, professional way to handle things. And while *Moesha* did depend a great deal on the chemistry of the ensemble, there was no doubt that the weight of the show was firmly on Brandy's shoulders. It was a big load for her to carry, but she was obviously managing it very well indeed.

One of the reasons it all worked so well was the fact that Brandy and her fictional counterpart were so similar. She'd recognized that when she first read the script, and now that the writers knew, it was even more so.

"Moesha takes things to heart, but she doesn't like to show it," Brandy observed. "I'm like that in a lot of ways. I take things from people and I won't talk about it. I'll talk about it with my mother and [best friend] Joi, and with my dad, but that's it. I don't show my feelings much to anyone."

Perhaps the biggest difference was that Moesha seemed to follow trends, although, ironically, what she'd wear onscreen, and the trademark braids, which Brandy had been wearing for a while, quickly began showing up on a lot of girls. In her own way, instead of being a follower, Moesha was a trendsetter, as art invaded life.

Nor was Brandy as social as Moesha, who always

seemed to be out and about, hanging somewhere or other. Brandy didn't have the time or the energy for that. Long days of filming left her exhausted, and her daily schedule was calculated to the minute, such were the demands on her time these days.

There were very few changes to *Moesha* between seasons. After all, why mess with a winning formula? Merlin Santana, who played the cheating Ohagi, Moesha's first love, left the cast to join the *Steve Harvey Show*. In his place came Fredo Starr as Quinton, better known as just Q, the new kid in school, and a rapper, who'd become Moesha's new love interest.

The season started at school, where the boys' annual "list" had come out. Thought it was no surprise to anyone that Kim had been given the Biggest Mouth award, Mo was none too happy to discover that she'd been credited with the biggest booty. She was out for revenge. First of all, though, she had to discover who'd authored the list. All the indicators seemed to point to Quinton, the new kid in class. Mo, Kim, and Niecy (Shar Jackson) decided to get their own back by coming up with their own "list." Unsurprisingly, Quinton and Hakeem seemed to top most of the categories. Finally Quinton decided to put a stop to things before they went *too* far. He sat down with Moesha and denied having anything to do with the list, and invited her out that night to see him perform at a club—apart from being a student, he was also a rapper. Moesha was none too sure at first, but allowed herself to be persuaded. In the end, she was glad, because seeing him in another context made her realize she was quickly getting quite smitten by him.

The new season looked as if it might have Moesha

getting into some tighter situations. Certainly the second episode had her flirting with breaking the law. She, Kim, Hakeem, Niecy, and Q—who was now established as Mo's boyfriend, even if her parents didn't know yet—went to a party in Beverly Hills. Nothing went smoothly, and Q ended up in jail. The only way to get him out on bail was for Moesha to use the credit card her father had given, the one she'd been told was strictly for emergencies. It wasn't the best start to the relationship, but it all got worse. Q offered to help by having his hacker friend Donny (Dale Godboldo, Jr., who been a regular on *The Mickey Mouse Club*) remove the charges from the bill Frank would see. Of course, Frank found out, and Mo was in big trouble. But that wasn't the only problem: having met Donny, Mo found herself very attracted to him. How could she tell Q, and what was she going to do about it?

From seriousness to silliness, the next show went to the other end of the scale, as Kim and Gabriella argued—violently—over who was Moesha's best friend. That was real enough, that sort of thing had happened in true life often. But it went way over the top when Mo tried to break up the fight and ended up out cold from an accidental punch.

Something Brandy had never expected was to be on television with her old friend Kobe Bryant. But that was exactly what happened when he appeared on *Moesha*. He was guesting as a basketball player who needed some tutoring to push up his SAT scores to an acceptable level, to actually make it into college, where his career might blossom. And it was Mo who had to do the tutoring. And why not? She was bright, a good student, with excellent grades. Without being preachy, the show made its point. All too often, athletes were pushed and encouraged in their sports, both at the high school and college levels, and allowed to just flow through the academic system without ever receiving what they really needed, which was a good education. Just because they received the appropriate pieces of paper didn't mean they were really qualified for anything.

The big show of the early season came during the November sweeps, actually on election night, November 5. To show its faith in the show, UPN had made *Moesha* the centerpiece of the night, with a big—*really* big—two-part episode. It all began with Mo winning four tickets to *MTV Megafest*, a concert packed with hip-hop and R&B stars. She invited Kim, Niecy, and Hakeem. Just before the show, however, she and Q got back together, but, with all her tickets promised, she couldn't invite him. That was no problem for Q, however. As usual, he had a plan that would make sure all five of them gained entry, then messed it up by bringing his four cousins—who made up a singing group (played by 112)—along. Before the show, Q met Moesha's parents for the first time, a meeting which didn't go too well for anybody, particularly the over-protective Frank, who saw any boyfriend of Moesha's as dangerous, particularly a rapper like Q.

Inevitably, the plan didn't work. Moesha found herself inside, and so did the group, but everyone else was still firmly outside the show, and without tickets. Q, who seemed to know everybody, finally managed to squeeze himself and Hakeem through the doors, because he happened to have an acquaintance going in (played by Lisa

Leslie, who'd been on the U.S. womens' basketball team which had won the Olympic gold medal) with her friend, and the guys posed as their escorts.

No sooner was he in than Mo spotted him—with another woman. It couldn't have happened at a worse time. She was chatting with Russell Simmons, the television producer who also owns Def Jam records, praising the talents of Q's cousins—and Simmons was interested.

Meanwhile, Kim and Niecy were still out in the cold, and having no luck trying to get in.

In part two, which aired half an hour later, a very unhappy Moesha, still mad at Q because of his "date," tried to make him jealous by telling him that singer Montell Jordan had been showing a lot of interest in her, but Q wasn't buying that. Hakeem, meanwhile, was discovering the joys of a free buffet, and Kim and Niecy encountered problem after problem as they tried to find their way into the venue, finally making it at the last minute.

It was time for Moesha and Q to sit down and have a heart-to-heart talk, which was exactly what they did. They managed to sort out and salvage their relationship through a little bit of honesty, and take it to a new level.

The real highlight of the episode, though, was the concert sequence, which employed a huge number of extras—four hundred in all. 112 ended up performing, but they were only one among many big names. Also strutting their stuff were BlackStreet, Soul for Real, Xscape, A Tribe Called Quest, MC Lyte (who'd been a friend of Brandy's rapping on the remix of "I Wanna Be Down"), and jazz legend Nancy Wilson.

All in all, the episode was star-studded. Apart from

all the bands, there were plenty of cameos. Montell Jordan and Russell Simmons played themselves, as did P.J. Butta, a DJ on Los Angeles station KKBT-FM, and MTV VJ Idalis. Jermaine Dupri was a waiter, Howard Hewitt a limo driver, Jo Marie Payton-Noble was Valerie Shaw, rapper Yo Yo was an usher, and Reggie McFadden played a security guard.

It was a very blatant attempt to woo a huge audience for the show, specifically a young audience, and it worked. The episodes were widely advertised on UPN and in print ads before the week. And it provided an entertaining alternative to the election results the big networks were carrying. It brought a lot of new viewers to the show, some of whom were bound to stay.

More than that, it was one of the biggest aggregations of black talent ever seen on television, which made it something of a landmark. If there was one thing wrong, it was that Brandy herself wasn't one of the singers, but in the context of the show, that simply wouldn't have worked; it wouldn't have been real. As it was, there was enough music to go around.

It was certainly the costliest and most ambitious episode of *Moesha* ever, in fact one of the most ambitious sitcom episodes ever, with so many extras and so many stars all working together to make it happen. But when the ratings appeared, it seemed that a strong dividend had been paid. *Moesha* was now firmly implanted in the consciousness of America.

After all that, the next couple of shows were almost bound to be low-key, and indeed they were. When Mo and her friends were trying to get a romantic evening alone with their boyfriends underway, it was Myles, whom Moesha was supposed to be babysitting, who kept halting the proceedings. Which was perhaps just as well, given that Frank still wasn't too happy about the idea of Moesha and Q being a couple and dating.

The following week saw Moesha taking on the responsibility of running The Den, as an injured Andell moved into the Mitchell house to recuperate from her accident. Mo had a chance to learn what running a business was all about, although on top of her schoolwork it proved to be quite a big job for her.

A tour in Arizona by the school basketball team offered Mo and her crew a chance to hit the road in "Road Trip," although that was just a part of the fun. The other half was the Mitchells—Frank, Dee, Mo, and Myles—celebrating their first Thanksgiving together as a family. It was an occasion everyone wanted to go perfectly, but, like all the best-laid plans, everything that could go wrong, did, although in the end the catalogue of disasters simply brought them closer than they'd been before.

Q and Mo were very definitely an item. In fact, she was spending a lot of time with him, much too much in Frank's estimation. He wanted her to get a job, which he believed would take her mind off her boyfriend, and she promised she'd find one. Instead of looking, though, she continued to give Q all her free time, to the point where she was skipping studying and homework to be with him. When her grades began to slip, that was the last straw for Frank. He'd reluctantly agreed to let her date him in the first place, but now it had to stop: School came before everything else. In an attempt to hold everything together, and for her dad to see that Q really wasn't a bad influence on her, she arranged for him to come over for dinner, so they could all meet and talk, and her family could see Q the way she did. In the end it didn't quite work that way—unlike her, neither Frank nor Dee ended up in love with him—but they did realize that he wasn't a bad kid, after all, and a compromise was reached, whereby Mo could still see him, if she kept her grades up. It wasn't perfect, but it was workable for them all.

The constant reinforcement, in a very gentle way, of all the positive values, was one of the delights of *Moesha* for a lot of parents. And, undoubtedly, it did help some kids study harder, or even stay in school, as Mo herself became more and more of a role model.

One thing that *Moesha* did, in a quiet way, was reinforce the Black Experience. Part of that was the Harlem Renaissance, the writers and artists who had been such a creative force in that part of New York earlier this century. To many it was little more than a phrase, and to others it was something they'd never even heard of before. The show put a human face on it when Mo discovered that one of the Mitchells' elderly neighbors, whom she'd simply thought of as another old woman, had actually been a part of that movement. She'd known all the key figures there, and lived the life. Through her, if she wanted to listen, Mo could learn about the culture, as well as the fact that the elderly are more than simply cranky old folk; they had pasts, often very interesting pasts, and many of them had played their own part in history. There was a great deal to be learned by listening to her elders.

Of course, like all sitcoms, *Moesha* continued to flip-flop between the serious and the silly, and it was back to the silly when Mo taught a dance class at the local elementary school. She enjoyed it, and the ten-year-old girls who were her students enjoyed having someone so fresh in charge for once. When Mo had to babysit Myles, she took him along to the class—against his will—and all the girls thought the was adorable. In turn, he wanted to join in with the dancing. While there, through one of those bizarre coincidences, he was spotted by a producer of commercials, who signed him up on the spot. That was the last thing Moesha, Frank, or Dee, needed. The sudden ''fame'' (even though he'd done nothing), went straight to Myles's head, and all of a sudden he was all attitude, which meant he was ripe for a fall, and that came soon enough.

Family and school came together in ways that weren't too pleasing for Moesha when Dee became the new vice principal at her school. Dee was firmly committed to academic excellence, no matter what it cost. Her popularity wasn't an issue. But when the grades of the some of the basketball team began to slip, and she pulled them off the team right before an important playoff game, that was taking things too far for Mo—especially as one of the players involved was Q. The students were angry, but Dee wasn't about to budge. And poor Mo was caught right in the middle between school and family, even though it was a family member she still hadn't fully accepted. In the end, Dee's defender was the least likely person—Q himself. Hoops were important, everyone knew that, but they were nowhere near as important as a good education, which could set you up for life, rather than for the next hour. It was a lesson for Q, for Dee, and for Moesha herself.

Reality reared its head the following week. There was a school trip being organized, one that Moesha really wanted to take, a trip to Africa. It was possibly a once-in-a-lifetime opportunity. However, it was also a once-in-a-lifetime cost. Though Frank and Dee wanted her to go, the simple fact of the matter was that they didn't have the money. It didn't matter how much she begged and pleaded, or how much she insisted she could learn there—they couldn't afford it. That was the bottom line, even if it took her a while to accept the fact and learn that in this life you couldn't always get what you wanted.

But there were always lessons to be learned, and plenty of food for thought. Moesha received more of both in the episode titled "Strike A Pose." Kim wanted Mo to model the clothes she'd designed in the "Face Of Tomorrow" contest. After much persuading, she agreed. At the same time, Moesha met Ladonna, a woman who owned a successful bookstore. It was an inspiration to her to begin reading more books written by women—of which there were certainly plenty. Slowly, a realization dawned upon her: that a woman's intellect was often ignored, with far too much emphasis placed on her looks and her body. That colored her attitude as she modeled Kim's clothes. But what Moesha had intended as disdain was interpreted by the judges as perfectly aloof, exactly the way a model should be—and all of a sudden, Mo found herself voted the Face of Tomorrow, exactly what she didn't want. Kim, on the other hand, thought that it was all due to her clothes, and took a stroll down the catwalk herself to celebrate her victory.

Was it art imitating life, or art inspiring life? It was

impossible to say. But at the end of the season, Brandy would become a model in real life. Not in ads, although those would come later, but a real fashion model. At five feet seven inches she was actually a little short, but with her look as she matured, and her poise, she was snapped up by the Wilhelmina agency, and flown to Milan, Italy, to stride up and down the runway wearing the latest Italian designs and pose for the cameras. And she did it, as everything else, with great style and dignity. You really had to end up wondering if there was anything Brandy couldn't do well. Singing, acting, modeling . . . what was there left for her to tackle?

That was a few months ahead. For now, there was still the second season of *Moesha* that needed to be the focus of her attention, and an episode that brought out one of the show's real in-jokes, namely that Moesha was tone-deaf, unable to sing a note. A minor detail like that, however, wasn't about to stop her wanting to sing backup on Q and Hakeem's demo tape, although they were considerably less certain about it than she was. In fact, they tried everything they could to dissuade her from helping them. On the home front, things were changing, too, as Dee, the school vice principal, decided to set an example by welcoming a French exchange student into the house, who certainly made a small difference in the lives of Mo and Myles, not to mention Frank.

Hakeem's birthday was coming. Mo had known him for many years, and she knew that one thing he wanted, although he never said it, was to be reunited with the father who'd left the family when he was a little kid, and whom he'd never seen since. The best present she could give her best friend was the thing he really wanted.

All she had to do was find his father, something that proved easier than she'd expected, once she began looking. Having found him (the father was played by Michael Ralph), she took it upon herself to invite him to the party. It was last thing Hakeem expected, to see his dad there, on this day, of all days. There was a lot of time to be made up, a lot of bonding to do. But that could wait for the future. For now, thanks to Moesha, they could enjoy the moment. Once again she'd proved herself to be a true friend to Hakeem.

Niecy hadn't really been a featured player during the season, more just a member of Mo's crew. But the next episode was all about her. She'd had boyfriends before, but had never experienced the real love thing. When she met Steve (Cory Tyler), she suddenly knew what she'd been missing. He was just as infatuated with her as she was with him. A couple of years older, he was about to graduate high school and already had his plans made for the future—he was going into the Army, where there were some real prospects for him, some training, and money for college. Impulsively, he proposed to Niecy, and equally impulsively, she accepted. This was real, it was now, and she was willing to give up everything—her family, her friends, her future, to be with Steve.

She wasn't the first, and she certainly wouldn't be the last, but her friends weren't too happy with the situation. They were pleased for her, but they wanted her to wait, even though that was highly unlikely to ever happen. In the end, of course, she did opt to stay home, and to complete her education before doing anything rash like that. In comparison, the secondary plot, with Frank and Dee wondering just what to do for their anniversary, semed like very small potatoes, the light counterpoint to the bigger serious subject.

The season was nearing an end, which meant that everything was building to a climax, and the thread would be the ongoing relationship between Moesha and Q. One thing they'd never had was a whole lot of time alone, so when Mo finally had the house to herself one night, Q was the perfect person to invite over, even though she knew she shouldn't. And one place they *definitely* shouldn't have ended up was in her bedroom, with the lights off, necking. But that was exactly what they did, and that was how Frank and Dee found them. Needless to say, it didn't sit too well with Mo's parents, and it didn't do much for the way they felt about Q, either, which had slowly been improving. She'd done exactly what they'd told her she couldn't do. And for blatantly ignoring the rules, she was grounded. Any dates with Q were totally out of the question. It was the price she paid for trying to put a little romance—innocent romance, at that, although Frank and Dee didn't believe it would have stayed innocent—into her life.

What she needed desperately was to get back in Frank's good graces, and to have her grounding cancelled. Mo's chance occured with the season finale. It was prom time, and all the girls were excited about it, except Moesha. She'd been looking forward to going with Q, and now that just wasn't going to happen—no way would her parents allow it. So it looked as if Mo would be missing out on the prom this year. Finally Frank offered an alternative. She could go, as long as she took Fraiser, the son of one of his friends. It was the only way she'd be able to go, so she agreed, as much to please her father as actually attend the prom. This being high school, the news that Moesha would be going with someone else soon reached Q. And being a boy, he naturally misinterpreted everything, and thought that Moesha had dumped him for someone new, right at the highlight of the year. He wanted revenge, and he got it. He broke up with her.

Their romance had lasted a year, and suddenly it was over—or so it seemed, as the season finished. Would they, could they, get back together? They'd seemed so perfectly suited, but a mix of circumstances and temper had blown them apart.

The second season of *Moesha* really capitalized on the base that had been established the year before. Brandy was able to bring more to the character in subtle ways, and the writers had been able to introduce some subtle storylines here and there (like the Harlem Renaissance episode, or the women's minds/women's bodies problem) to offer an audience something to chew on between the jokes. *Moesha* had found its audience, and was sitting comfortably in the ratings, with only *Star Trek: Voyager* to challenge it as UPN's top show.

It had made Brandy into a multimedia star. No one thought of her now as a singer who'd tried her hand at comedy. If anything, it was the other way around these days. She was accepted as an actress in her own right. At eighteen years of age, the girl was a bona fide star.

While there were a lot of similarities between Brandy and Moesha, there was one big difference—Mo had started dating at sixteen, and Brandy still had two more years to wait, until her eighteenth birthday in February, 1997.

"You never know about guys today," she said. Which was probably true. But it was impossible not to think she was yearning for the day when she also said, "I have friends who are guys that I hang out with, but no one has come up yet to the house to pick me up. I am still waiting for that."

She might be a big name, but that certainly didn't mean she had to act like one. "I want to feel like I'm approachable," Brandy explained, "like people can reach out and touch me. I want people to feel like I'm their sister."

A lot of the drive that pushed her was a mix of insecurity and competition.

"Insecurity's a good thing. I always think the next person doesn't like me, so it makes me work even harder." That was one half of the equation. The other was to be better than anyone else, to be known. "I want success. I want it all. If I die today, I want people to talk about me on every channel."

The image of that might have been a bit gruesome, but it made sense. It was the feeling that made someone into a star, that forced them to put out a hit album, to act on a hit show, to strain themselves to try and do everything. It was a quality common to every top performer, really, that burning *desire* to have it all, to see their faces on posters, their name in print, themselves on television. Some had it, most didn't—or not enough of it to want it so badly that it became their aim in life, followed singlemindedly.

And it seemed that you were either born with it or

you weren't. Brandy had been. From the first time she was two and stood up in church to sing, she'd known that that was what she wanted, what she *needed* in her life. And she'd gone for it, with her parents' blessing and backing.

Now she was eighteen. Two seasons of *Moesha* were behind her. She was an adult now, legally able to make all her own decisions. The future was wide open ahead of her. She could do anything she wanted. The label was clamoring for another record. UPN wanted another season of its favorite sitcom. Brandy had it made. But right now, the season over, she had some free time ahead of her, a dangerous thing for a workaholic. She needed something to fill all those weeks over the early summer. What would she do, what could she find?

nine

By now, it was fully two-and-a-half years since *Brandy* had appeared and been such a major sensation. In terms of music, a great deal had happened since then. By any standards, Brandy should have been back in the studio, working furiously to put the finishing touches on her next album.

She was at least slowly beginning work on it. She'd made excuses as long as she could. Sonja Norwood said, "[O]nce it started to take too long, we told her she needed to get back in the studio."

To that end, Paris Davis and Craig Kallman moved from New York to Los Angeles for a few months to work with her. They both worked in the A&R (Artist and Repertoire) department at Atlantic Records, and had been assigned the special responsibility for this new project after Darryl Williams, the man who'd signed her to the label, moved on.

It was an indication of just how big they believed Brandy was, that they were willing to give her this very special treatment. She was so nervous about the idea of a second record that it took Davis and Kallman coming to her house, and sitting down with Brandy and her family, to convince her that it was a good idea.

And it definitely was a brilliant idea. With the profile of Brandy Norwood very high, thanks to *Moesha*, it was quite likely that a second album would easily outsell the first, no small task. That made it worth all the time and effort to have Brandy prepared, relaxed, and confident.

She wanted more involvement this time around, to have more of a hand in the writing of the songs, and of the way they sounded. There was no problem with that. Brandy was older, it was natural she wanted to spread her wings a little bit, and be more than just the singer.

They had to decide on producers, and two names that kept coming up were Rodney Jerkins and Fred Jerkins III. They wouldn't be the only people used, but Brandy got along well with them, well enough to begin writing some new material. Maybe it was still taking baby steps, but a new Brandy album was slowly happening.

But just as it seemed as if that would be her focus for the summer, Brandy was offered another project. And once again the instigator was Whitney Houston. After working together on the *Waiting to Exhale* soundtrack, Whitney had kept in touch with the young singer, offering advice about life, a career, everything. Brandy couldn't quite think of her as a friend because "I don't think I can ever be friends with a star because I'm so starstruck. Every time she calls me, I scream."

And now Whitney was calling again. She'd been developing an idea for television, a remake of the Rodgers and Hammerstein musical, *Cinderella*, based on the fairy tale. This was a very big deal, with Disney involved, who'd committed to airing it on the *Wonderful World of*

Disney on ABC. As well as being executive producer, Whitney would also be acting, along with some other big names, like Whoopi Goldberg, Bernadette Peters, and Jason Alexander (George on *Seinfeld*). What Whitney wanted to know was, would Brandy be interested in taking the title role and playing Cinderella?

Of course, there was no way she could turn down an opportunity like that, and not just because it was Whitney doing the asking. It would offer a challenge that went beyond acting, beyond the kind of singing she was known for, and push her more as an all-around entertainer, rather than leave her pigeonholed in R&B.

The snag was that working on *Cinderella* would mean she couldn't focus solely on her new album. The completion date would have to be pushed back, and there'd be no way it could end up released by Christmas 1997. That would mean missing out on a lot of potential sales as Christmas presents. But if *Cinderella* was as good as it should be, that might not matter in the long run. It would reaffirm Brandy in the eyes of the public as a singer.

Now she was eighteen, Brandy was ready to take charge of some aspects of her life. Not all, by any means. Although she could easily afford a place of her own, she had no desire to move away from her parents.

"When you live alone you have to do everything yourself," she reasoned. "I don't want the full responsibility of taking out the trash, and if I'm hungry, I can just call my dad, 'Dad, go get me something to eat.'"

And what would he bring her? Well, if she was lucky, it would be one of her favorites, a jelly-and-fried-egg sandwich, which she'd loved since she was a kid.

She was happy to keep to the curfew set by her parents for 2 A.M., and to follow their dictum to be polite to people. Sonja was still her mother *and* her manager, and that certainly wasn't going to change.

Brandy had a car, a Range Rover, and that gave her the freedom she needed in Los Angeles.

And she'd also had a boyfriend.

It had been brewing for a long time, really, since 1995 to be exact, when she'd been on tour with Boys II Men and become friends with Wayna Morris. Granted, he was five years older than her, but they connected; there seemed to be a bond between them. At that stage, though, there was never any question of them being more than friends. He was on the road constantly, Brandy was busy promoting her album and preparing for *Moesha*, and their schedules never seemed to coincide. Besides, Brandy had yet to reach the magical age of eighteen, when she would finally date.

Things began to change at her eighteenth birthday party, which was held at the house of Blues, on Sunset Boulevard in West Hollywood, L.A.

"She called me," Morris explained, "and she said, 'You gotta come to my party,' and I said, 'I'm there.'"

He was one of many guests, including Kobe Bryant, who, Brandy insisted, had always been "just a friend." There was Penny Hardaway from the Orlando Magic, Jaleel White of *Family Matters*, classmates from Pepperdine, where Brandy was still going through her freshman year (as if she didn't have enough to fill her time), and most of the cast of *Moesha*, with one of two notable exceptions, not to mention, of course, her family.

The crowd made her happy.

"All my favorite stars, my family and my friends are here. I'm having the happiest birthday that an eighteen-year-old could ever have," Brandy said.

The best part, though, was Morris, who stuck close to her. It had been obvious to everyone that they'd get together once she began dating, and that was exactly what happened. The transition from friends to boyfriend and girlfriend seemed quite smooth at first. They'd already shared a great deal, and now they were able to share even more.

The road of true love, however, didn't always run smooth, not even for someone like Brandy. After a few months together, they split up. Maybe it was the pressures of the business, or maybe it was something more personal; the full reasons were never given, and they didn't need to be; it was a purely private matter. It wasn't easy for Brandy, though, saying goodbye to her first boyfriend, and a lot of what she was feeling would be reflected in the lyrics she wrote for her new album. Indeed, to express those feelings was one of the reasons she wanted to co-write a number of the songs.

"I've gone through that, you know, breaking up with him, my first love," she said. "I was really heartbroken. I was sick, and it was hard, really hard, but I got through it. I'm okay now. I miss him, but I'm okay."

It wasn't as if she was moving from one guy straight to another. This had been a very big deal for her, and she'd need time to heal, probably a lot of time for her heart to mend before she could even think about falling in love with someone else. Besides, with the workload she had to carry during the summer, there wasn't even the time to think about meeting someone new. There were the rehearsals for *Cinderella*, all the pre-production on her new record. She was back to a full schedule.

But she wasn't the only one in the family working on her music. Her little brother, Ray J., had also been busy in that area. Like her, he'd signed with Atlantic, and been working on his own record, using some of the same people who'd contributed to the success of *Brandy*. He'd never wanted to trade on her name to help his career. Professionally, he wasn't Brandy's brother—he was simply Ray J., to stand or fall on his own merits.

Understandably, he too was managed by his mom, keeping it all in the family, but she was doing as good a job for him as she'd done for his sister.

He'd concentrated on his acting for a long time, having been L.J. on *Sinbad*, had a role in the 1994 HBO special, *The Enemy Within*, and appeared on the BET presentation *When We Were Colored*, a small part in *Mars Attacks* and *Steel* (which starred the mighty Shaq). And then there were all the commercials—for McDonalds, Denny's, Nintendo, and even Disney. But music had always had a place in his heart.

"Even though my sister started a lot earlier than me, I always knew I would get a chance to show the singer inside of me," he said.

And his first real chance had come a couple of years before, when he'd been an opening act on the Brandy and Boyz II Men tour, even without an album to his name. He'd appeared at the prestigious Apollo Theater in New York (as his sister had before him), and in *Twist*, a musical that enjoyed an off-Broadway run. And all this before he was even fifteen!

But 1997 saw all the musical seeds coming into bloom as he released *Everything You Want*, his first album. Like his sister, he was assured and mature, even on a debut recording. If it didn't make quite the same dent in the charts as *Brandy*, it still didn't do too badly, with two singles that did surprisingly well on the R&B charts.

More importantly, it boded well for a long career ahead, and a pair of kids to make their parents proud. Sonja and Willie had spotted the talent in their kids and nurtured it to fruition. That they both had music in their veins was hardly surprising, given Willie's talent, but that they'd both managed to make careers for themselves as actors was perhaps a bit of a surprise. And the odds against them having achieved the success they'd managed were quite astounding.

Ray J. might not be the big star that Brandy already was, but he was still two years younger than her, and had time on his side. And, in many ways, he'd achieved more earlier than she had, what with his television resume. He was someone who was obviously going places, even if he wasn't yet old enough to drive. He was his sister's best friend and confidant, and he was not just walking in her footsteps; he was very definitely treading his own path, on the way to becoming a star in his own right.

Everything You Want was obviously what was occupying him during 1997, as Brandy turned eighteen and saw everything in her life really taking off for the stratosphere. He played shows and promoted the record, and had every reason to feel proud it had done so well, and that his sister and parents were there for him, every single step of the way.

* * *

Budgeted at $18 million, *Cinderella* was going to be a extravaganza of a television show. Making musicals for television, and particularly one of the big three networks, wasn't something that generally amounted to good business, but it wasn't often that something came along that starred Whitney Houston, Whoopi Goldberg, *and* Brandy, three of the most popular African-American women in show business, all proven draws in their own right, and major draws at that.

The idea of just ignoring the differences of race was inspired, something a post-Rodney King America sorely needed. But if that was a message, there was no reference to it in the finished product, and there didn't need to be. With songs by Rodgers and Hammerstein, who'd written some of the great musicals of the century, it didn't need any kind of point to push home. Existing as entertainment, which is how most people would view it, anyway, was more than enough.

Organizing everything was important, obviously, but so were singing rehearsals for the cast. This was rather different from the pop music Whitney and Brandy were used to signing, and required a more applied technique, and plenty of practice, working with a vocal coach to be able to capture all the nuances.

For Brandy, the chance to work with the woman she'd already called "her fairy godmother" (and who would, in this, be quite literally that) was like a dream coming true. They'd met, and they'd talked—well, Whitney had talked; Brandy has listened—but this seemed huge. It was the biggest production she'd ever taken part in, much more sumptuous than *Moesha*, and requiring a lot of her in the title role. But Whitney was certain that Brandy could handle it. She wouldn't have asked her otherwise.

"She is Cinderella," Houston said. "Brandy knows what she wants, and she goes for it, just like Cinderella. She has a drive."

Maybe the older woman saw her younger self mirrored in Brandy. Maybe she just saw someone whose talent she appreciated. Whatever the reason, this was the second big break she'd given Brandy, and it was received with gratitude.

But Brandy's status had also been earned. She'd worked very hard, for most of her life, to be where she now was. All those gigs that had played when she was younger, wondering if she'd ever go anywhere, were reaping their rewards. The brief appearances in *Arachnophobia* and *Demolition Man*, even the season of *Thea*, had been like apprenticeships, where she'd learned all the ropes of performing and been allowed to refine her natural abilities. and performing with Whitney gave her impetus for working on her own new record. Here she was, with one of the biggest. Brandy had it in her to be another one of the biggest, in due course. Everything fed into everything else; that was the way of life. So it was with a light heart she began the hard work and long days of filming *Cinderella*.

Offering prime-time America a traditional Broadway-style musical in the late 1990s was a daring gesture, even when the story was something as classic as *Cinderella*. For much of the potential viewing audience the idea was outdated. But it relied on the proven appeal of its cast—

specifically Whitney and Brandy—to draw people in.

There was no doubt that the story itself was timeless, the perfect rags-to-riches tale that everyone had loved and wanted for themselves at one time or another. Add to that some big names and extravagant special effects, and you had yourself a musical, nineties-style.

Everyone knew Whitney and Brandy could sing. Perhaps the biggest surprise of all was Jason Alexander. While his face was well-known as George from *Seinfeld,* very few knew him outside that context, and hardly anyone would have guessed that he could not only be funny, but also sing—and dance. Even Whoopi Goldberg proved herself more than capable of carrying a tune. But for actors of a certain age, the ability to do everything on a stage had almost been a necessity if they were going to keep working.

As co-executive producer, Whitney had her name above the title, and an appearance at the beginning, before any of the action, dressed in a glamorous, skin-tight sheath, beautifully made-up, her hair in corkscrew curls, every inch the fairy godmother she was portraying, full of magic.

All eyes, however, would be on Brandy, as poor Cinderella, treated terribly by her wicked stepmother (Bernadette Peters), and her awful stepsisters, Calliope (Veanne Cox), and Minerva (Natalie Desselle). While they shopped in the town, she was left in the street, holding packages, and singing to herself about her ideal man, as a Punch and Judy show captured her attention.

What she didn't know was that the Prince (Paolo Montalban) was also there, singing about his ideal woman. He was dressed like an ordinary person, incognito, a man looking for love.

When the one of the royal coaches almost ran Cinders down, it was the Prince, this mysterious stranger, who helped pick up the packages, and he and Cinders began to talk—until she was finally called away by her stepmother.

Back at the palace, the Queen (Whoopi Goldberg) was organizing a ball, which would invite all the eligible women in the kingdom, so her son might marry. He, however, wasn't so keen, and it was only thanks to the head servant, Lionel (Jason Alexander), that it was going to happen.

Cinders, meanwhile, was at home, with demands coming from her stepmother and stepsisters. While they lived a luxurious life, Cinderella had to do all the work, with only the kitchen as her sanctuary, where she could dream her dreams of the future. She wanted to leave, but she was scared.

The preparations for the ball were elaborate—lots of food, decorations—and contained the best choreography of the film, by Rob Marshall. The announcement went out across the land, requesting the presence of all single young ladies to meet the Prince.

The Prince had his doubts whether this scheme of his mother's would work, but he came to a compromise with the Queen and the King (Victor Garber): If he didn't find the girl of his dreams at the ball (and he truly didn't believe he would), then he'd be able to seek her his way, to look for someone he could really love.

The stepmother and her two daughters were excited about the ball. She felt, in her scheming way, sure she could end up marrying one or other of them to the Prince. But what of love, Cinders wanted to know. This was about marriage, not love, was the reply, and a cue for the best-known song of the night, "Falling in Love With Love," whose lyrics had actually been written by Lorenz Hart, not Oscar Hammerstein II, sung by Bernadette Peters, as she vamped around the house.

Calliope and Minerva, of course, were not exactly the greatest catches in the world, both utterly devoid of good taste and good sense. Minerva wanted to charm the Prince by reciting poetry, while Calliope hoped to charm him with her laugh, which always ended up as a snort. Their chances were slim, but she had to push them anyway. And so, dressed in the most appalling gowns, they left for the palace and the ball, to join all the other hopefuls.

Every young girl in the kingdom was going—except for Cinderella. She was, as her stepmother had told her, common, and nowhere near good enough for a young man of royal blood. All she could do was wish.

But wishes can come true, especially when you have a fairy godmother appear outside the window. But Whitney was playing a very down-to-earth fairy godmother, one who thought wishes and dreams were fine, but if you spent too much time dreaming, and not enough putting them into action, nothing would ever happen. Along with the fulfilment of her wishes came a pep talk for Cinderella, the girl who'd always been treated badly, and whose self-esteem was low.

Thanks to the magic of special effects, a pumpkin became a coach before our very eyes, and mice were transformed into horses and coachmen. And Cinderella herself—already beautiful, of course, with her long braids and perfect face—became a vision of loveliness in an off-the-shoulder gown, her hair up, held in place by a diamond tiara. She was no longer Cinderella, she was a princess. At least, that was what those who saw her would assume. The only thing she had to remember was to leave the ball by midnight, when the magic would wear off.

At the palace, the ball was moving along. The Prince had promised to dance with every girl, and indeed he did, although the stepsisters had had to be dragged off him. It was tedium; there was no one who struck his fancy.

Until someone appeared at the top of the staircase.

She was, as the saying goes, a vision of loveliness, and he knew immediately that this was the girl for him. She slowly walked down, looking a little shy and embarrassed at all the attention, and then the Prince took her into his arms and they began to glide around the floor. Whereas the other girls had been lucky to enjoy five seconds in his company, the Prince wasn't about to let this girl go. Everyone wondered who she could be, although the stepmother thought her face looked a little familiar.

The King and Queen were happy that their boy seemed to have found someone.

They danced in the ballroom, they danced out on the terrace, and they danced in the garden, before going back inside, where first the King talked to this girl, and then the Queen, who asked about her family—a topic Cinders definitely didn't want to discuss. She ended up running back into the garden, where the Prince found her, and they talked. He was in love, that was obvious, and so was she.

The stepsisters were hiding behind bushes, following them around, wondering just who this lovely girl was, never thinking for a minute it could be their own sister.

Finally, just as the Prince was about to propose, the clock began to strike midnight, and Cinders had no option but to leave. She ran through the ballroom, back out into the town, where she was transformed into a servant in rags, her gorgeous pumpkin coach a mere pumpkin again, the footmen and horses were once more mice scurrying to freedom.

The Prince followed, but he couldn't find her. All that was left was a glass slipper that had fallen off as she ran down the steps. He didn't even know her name.

He'd met her and lost her, and now he was determined to find her again. In the morning he and Lionel would set off with the glass slipper and try it on every female foot in the kingdom. The one it fitted would become his bride.

Cinderella had run home to be there before her family arrived back from the ball. She'd asked them about it, pretending that she'd never gone, although when she began to tell how she imagined the palace to be, it raised plenty of suspicions in the mind of her stepmother. Both Minerva and Calliope insisted that they'd each spent an hour with the Prince, and their mother believed he might well pick one of them for his wife, although she knew, really, that would never happen. Inside she knew that the mysterious girl was her stepdaughter.

Lionel and the Prince traveled all over the kingdom,

going from foot to foot to foot, but never finding the girl whose foot was a perfect fit for the slipper. Cinders, meanwhile, had determined to leave home. Her late father had asked her to stay, but she realized that she couldn't. Staying meant living in a world of dreams, rather than living her own life. She packed up what few belongings she had in her own little corner of the world, her kitchen.

That was when the royal party arrived for glass slipper fittings. The stepmother, knowing that Cinders was the one, locked her in the kitchen, and hid the key. Both Calliope and Minerva's feet were far too large and ungainly for the slipper. Even their mother tried it on, and actually got her foot in it, but the fit was painfully tight.

The Prince asked what lay behind the door they all seemed to be trying to hide, and finally they let him into the kitchen. But the room was empty. Cinderella had left. She hadn't gone far, however. She was just at the gate, where the royal coach had scared her. Immediately he saw her, the Prince knew this was her. He put two and two together, that the simple girl he'd met in the town square and his princess were one and the same, and that was confirmed when the slipper fit as if it had been made for her—which it had been, of course. From there it was a whirlwind of wedding preparations, of true love, and the ceremony of the century in the kingdom, with everyone invited, except the stepmother and her two daughters, who were left outside the locked gates. Everyone who deserved to lived happily ever after.

It was a grand production, probably the glitziest, most glamorous version of *Cinderella* ever. The sets were lavish, hundreds of extras and dancers were employed. Veanne Cox and Natalie Desselle were superb as the light comic relief of the stupid sisters, and Bernadette Peters almost hissed her way through the role of the stepmother. Whoopi Goldberg squeaked a lot as the Queen, and Paolo Montalban was effortlessly natural and charming as the Prince who yearned for true love.

But it was Brandy who held it all together, portraying the innocence and loveliness of Cinderella. She was perfectly suited for the role, naturally lovely to look at, and with an innate modesty that became her character. For anyone who'd wondered how she'd make the transition from R&B to show tunes, the answer was—easily. There was a sweetness in her voice that made all Cinderella's plaintive desire come alive, and her naturally low pitch made it all seem intimate, rather than staged.

"My best friends that are my age, they think I'm singing opera," she laughed. "But they think it's beautiful."

And beautiful was the word to sum up everything about *Cinderella*. Whitney had staked a lot by putting her name to this, but the end product was everything she could have hoped, and Brandy more than fulfilled every expectation that could have been placed upon her. It added another dimension to her, truly moving her into the spotlight as an entertainer, one who'd shown she could do anything she set her mind to.

With its large budget, this version of *Cinderella* needed a big audience, and every effort was made to see that it received one. It was widely advertised, it was an *event*. The show aired on Sunday, November 2, 1997, on ABC's *The Wonderful World of Disney*. Everyone involved was hopeful, and already proud of the work they'd put into this. Still, no one could have anticipated the results that came out a few days later. Across the United States, more than thirty million viewers had tuned in to watch it. That was more than just another show; that was a phenomenon. It was ABC's highest-rated show of the week, beating out traditional favorites like *20/20*. It was a success, and so was Brandy, who'd rapidly become a household name. People who might never have bought one of her albums, maybe never even heard one of her songs, knew who she was now.

By the time it aired, she had already been back at work on *Moesha* for a few months. *Cinderella*, along with a lot of the work on her album, had been her summer vacation. But a change was as good as a rest. She'd learned things, she'd tried her hand at something new and conquered another field.

Exhausting as all the rehearsals and the filming schedule might have been, it was the kind of thing that left her energized, ready to take on more and more, which was just as well, because she had plenty to do.

Throughout the summer she'd shuttled back and forth between the studio lot where *Cinderella* was being filmed and the recording studio, having to get her head into a different space on each trip.

She'd changed. The person who'd started work on *Moesha* a couple of years before, the singer who'd recorded *Brandy*, they seemed like little girls to her now, far away. She'd grown up, she'd matured and really become her own person. Her life had been full of experiences. She'd been on the catwalk, she'd sung in front of thousands of people. Millions watched her every week.

Inside she was still the same normal girl she'd always

been. She still loved to go shopping, although the chances were fewer and fewer, given how busy she was. Her favorite video was *Clueless*. Her real friends remained the people she'd known a long time, people she trusted, who she could talk to quite easily, who weren't awed by her. She still loved her family and spent most of her free time with them. But there was another side of her now, the girl who hung out with Mariah Carey and Puff Daddy, who was invited to all the best parties and shows and given the VIP treatment when she attended. And still her feet remained squarely on the floor.

Now the third season of *Moesha* was waiting for her. Her album would soon be complete. She felt as if she was just beginning another phase in her career. And she was.

Ten

For the third season of *Moesha*, there were definite changes in the air. For a start, Mo was changing schools, from Crenshaw High to the private and rather upscale Bridgewood, where Frank believed she'd get a better education. And what about the relationship she and Q had shared? It had fizzled at the end of the previous season; would it return, or would they both move on?

The change of school was a good idea, since it allowed the writers to bring in some new characters and situations, fresh blood to the show. Not that the core didn't work—quite the opposite. But this avoided any possibilities of storylines becoming stale and recycled.

If anyone needed a indication of the respect UPN had for *Moesha*, it was evident with the early start to the season (August 26, 1997), and the fact that it kicked off with two new episodes, back-to-back, something to keep all of Brandy's fans happy.

Bridgewood was introduced as the school Mo was going to start attending in about a week. Frank wanted his daughter to have the best possible education, even if it meant stretching the Mitchell budget as tight as it could go. Moesha wasn't too sure. To her, the school resembled a prison, and she was certain it was going to be full of boring rich kids.

She'd just finished a long summer as a camp counselor. All she wanted to do was chill a little and hang with her friends, catch up on everything. More than anything, she was looking forward to the Labor Day concert, where Dru Hill would be performing. There, she was sure, she'd run into Q. What might happen, she had no idea, but she'd been thinking about him all summer. Frank, however, had other ideas for the holiday; all the family, and he meant *all*, was going to a fundraiser at Bridgewood.

Mo, expecting to hate every minute of the event, and all the people there, soon made a new friend in Haley (Dru Mouser), a student at the school who also wanted to escape and see the show. Together they did exactly that, catching the band as they performed two songs, "Tell Me" and "Never Make a Promise." With someone like Haley around, Mo was willing to concede that Bridgewood might not be quite as bad as she'd imagined. And when she did see Q, and their relationship rekindled, albeit as friends, everything seemed as if it might be all right.

The episode that followed directly didn't continue the storyline, oddly enough. Instead, it gave a completely unrelated story of sibling rivalry. Not between Mo and Myles, but between Frank Mitchell and his brother, Bernie.

Their father, Mo's paternal grandfather (Hal Williams), was visiting from Georgia. While the kids were glad to see him again, Frank found it difficult to be quite as happy. His dad had always preferred brother Bernie to him. It had been that way when they were children, and it still seemed to be that way, no matter what he did, no matter how successful he became. Somehow, Frank just couldn't seem to satisfy his father.

A week later, Moesha began the new school year at Bridgewood, and it proved, for the most part, to be exactly as she'd feared. She had a friend in Haley, but that seemed to be the only good thing about the place. A lot of the students *were* snobbish and cliquey, and regarded Mo as something of an upstart, common. One in particular, May Ellen (Monica McSwain), seemed intent on crossing swords with Mo—a very dangerous thing to do, as she found out. And her background at public school meant that one of her teachers had grave doubts about whether she should be enrolling in Advanced Placement history. She had to prove herself—and she did.

But going to Bridgewood was proving to be a no-win situation for Moesha. It hadn't been her idea; she'd been given no real choice in the matter. She couldn't wait to go home and hang with her real friends from Crenshaw. However, they accused her of becoming snobbish herself, simply by going to a private school, and it took her a long time to convince them that wasn't the case, that she was still exactly the same Mo they'd always known, and that was who she'd continue to be.

It was going to be an ongoing storyline for the season, a subtext of the way Mo was pulled between different parts of herself. School was important, but she didn't like where she was, even if the education was superior. Her friends remained a little suspicious of her. She was growing, and finding herself pulled between her two halves, the Mo who wanted to grow up, and the one who simply wanted to be who she'd always been, with her old friends.

But there were all kinds of tensions among the crew. One of the biggest came in the Halloween show, when Kim overheard her friends making jokes about her weight. That simply wasn't going to be allowed to happen, which was why she ended up at the Halloween party (dressed, quite aptly, as a she-devil) without the company of either Mo or Niecy.

Meanwhile, Moesha (costumed as Tina Turner) and Q, on their way to the party, found themselves trapped in a supernatural Halloween nightmare of sorts. Weird things were happening, and wouldn't stop happening. It was enough to terrify them both, even the normally cool Q. In the end, of course, everything was sorted out. Kim, Mo, and Niecy were friends again (even if, in real life, Brandy and Countess Vaughn were far from close), and they were able to come up with rational explanations for all the strange things that had happened to Mo and Q. Or could they . . . ?

It was light relief in a season that would see *Moesha* focus much more on the real, and Mo herself wanting to spread her wings a little more, and become her own person, rather than Frank Mitchell's daughter. The focus was much more on Mo herself, rather than her friends, or even her family.

However, friends would feature strongly in the episode called "Ryhthm and Dues." Although, in the end the tone-deaf Mo hadn't sung backup on Q and Hakeem's demo tape, Kim had, and Moesha was doing everything she could to make sure it was heard by as many people as possible. Finally she persuaded a local radio station to play it, with a good response, and soon there was a gig booked. But along with the great news came something bad—a cease-and-desist order. It seemed that Q and Hakeem had sampled a riff from a Morris Day song, and the man himself wasn't too happy about the sample being used without clearance or payment. He intended to sue, and nothing Mo could say would stop him.

Meanwhile, Q, Hakeem, and Kim were equally adamant that no lawsuit was going to stop them from performing the song, the one everyone seemed to love, when they appeared in front of an audience. All of Moesha's arguments just fell flat. She was stuck in the middle and no one was listening to her.

Bad became worse when Day, who'd first come to prominence as the lead singer for the Time, one of the great bands of the eighties, showed up at the gig. Now what was going to happen? Mo tried the only tactic left—flattery. And a little of it went a long way. Day, pleased to hear that the riff had been borrowed simply because they were all such big fans of his, backed off a little. Then a lot. No longer was there talk of lawsuits, much to Mo's relief. But even she hadn't expected what happened next. As the band began to perform the song, it wasn't the sample that played the riff, it was Day himself, singing it a capella, and completely bringing the house down.

This season saw the introduction of several new characters, but none had the impact of Usher. He was already an R&B star, like Brandy herself, when he joined the cast, and just a year older than her. And *Moesha* seemed to be just the beginning of an acting career for him. His recurring character, Jeremy, would date Mo. That done, Usher moved on to the soaps, appearing in seven episodes of the CBS series *Bold and the Beautiful*, before returning to singing as the opening act on Janet Jackson's 1998 summer tour, following a huge hit, "My Way," in the *Billboard* singles charts. As if that wasn't enough for one year, he'd also filmed his first feature, *The Faculty*, for release in December 1998, leading to questions about whether he'd be simply too busy to return to *Moesha*.

Perhaps his biggest episode of the season was when he and Mo ended up at a club with Q and his date, Tammy (played by singer/actress Maia Campbell). Not only that, they were seated at the same table in Club Unplugged to see singer Kenny Lattimore, who would perform his hit, "For You."

It was a difficult and embarrassing situation, but it had an odd result. Seeing him with someone else, Mo realized she was still attracted to Q and the feeling appeared to be mutual. They decided to try dating again, to see if they could make it work this time. It was quickly apparent that they couldn't, however. All the things that had broken them up before seemed to loom very tall this time around. There was simply no chance of romance between them any more. Maybe they knew each other too well for that, and they couldn't recapture the magic that had once existed. What they could do, and decided was the right thing, was to be friends, to be happy for each other and to help each other.

By now Q had become a character on the show in his own right. No longer just Mo's boyfriend, he was as much a regular as Kim, Niecy, or Hakeem, part of the crew, which was a good decision, as it opened up some interesting story avenues. This one, in particular, worked well, showing that people who'd once been in love could still remain friends. Breaking up didn't have to mean breaking off all contact and losing someone special.

Q's big episode had come the week before, when he attended a father-son retreat, at which Frank and Myles were also guests. Finally, there, Frank and Q would come to some sort of understanding and acceptance of each other. Frank had been scared of Q as the boy who might take his daughter away from him. This gave him a chance to see the real person, still young, with his own hopes and dreams for the future. To Mo, who'd become so used to the antagonism between them, this new situation was confusing, and not especially comfortable. Instead of a peacemaker, she felt like an intruder between the two of them.

Not that the girls didn't have their own thing going on while all the guys were bonding. The Den had been used as a set for a movie, and the price was a self-defense class for all the ladies, run by Don "The Dragon" Wilson (playing himself), a celebrity martial arts teacher. It was a good idea—good for all women, anywhere—giving them the opportunity to learn to defend themselves in a number of situations.

It was an interesting show, and quite notable for some of its guests. Among those attending the retreat was Charles, the boy who seemed to have the ideal father. When the credits rolled, Charles proved to be none other than Ray J., guesting on his sister's show. And one of the fathers was played by Lawrence Hilton-Jacobs, best known for the role of Washington in the 1970s sitcom, *Welcome Back, Kotter.*

As the season progressed, Mo still didn't feel that settled at Bridgewood. She tried to fit in and become part of the student body, but it wasn't easy—and her fiercely independent streak didn't help matters. She applied to join the staff of the school newspaper, but found herself rejected. Something like that wasn't going to stop her journalistic ambitions. Instead, she decided to start her own alternative Bridgewood paper, one that would tell the truth about the place.

That was all well and good, but she didn't realize just how much she was biting off in the project. Doing virtually everything herself meant that every minute of her time was taken up with the paper, at the expense of friends . . . and schoolwork, something she couldn't afford to neglect, not when she was trying to prove she was smarter than the rich kids. Mo had no life, and if she wasn't careful, she wouldn't even have a school career. In the end, it couldn't last, but in taking a stand, she'd shown to herself and to the other students, exactly what she was made of.

Those journalistic ambitions came to the fore again a week later. Frank's old friend, Alexandra Norris (Arthel Neville) had gone on to great things, becoming a White House correspondent for one of the big news organizations. That was something Mo could see herself doing in the future, becoming a famous, big-time reporter. Everything began with small steps, though, and she had real hopes that Norris, knowing her goals, would recommend her for an internship on Capitol Hill, where she could begin to learn the ins and outs of government and get to know people who might be able to help her in the future.

There was only one fly in the ointment—Norris might be an old friend of Frank's, but it was obvious to Moesha that her idea of friendship was a little more intimate than his. Frank was happily married, and Mo didn't want anything ruining his relationship with Dee (whom she'd finally accepted as a mother and a friend). Even if it meant losing her coveted internship, she wasn't going to let that happen. Finally, Mo confronted Norris about it all. It was a big risk, but one she felt she had to take for the sake of her family.

These were big issues, but ones well worth exploring. However, this was a season of Moesha grappling with big issues, as she grew up and began taking charge of her own life (and sometimes the lives of people around her). Not everything she tried would be successful, but if she didn't make the attempt, she'd never know. And underlying it all were the family values, the moral center that remained at the heart of the show and had made it so popular with kids *and* parents. It was all a big build to the finale, however, where everything would explode.

Things had definitely changed for Moesha. A season ago a co-ed slumber party would have been unthinkable, but now it was happening, *with* the blessing of the Mitchells. One thing they definitely didn't approve of was Mo's tattoo, which she acquired, very stupidly, on a bet.

"I wouldn't have done that," Brandy admitted, "especially on a dare when that's not what I really want to do."

And Mo regretted it immediately, but getting a tattoo

and getting rid of one were two very different things. The episode, along with the slumber party, came during the May ratings sweeps, and gave *Moesha* a twenty percent rise in female viewers, pushing the show above *JAG* with teens.

The climax, though, was the huge argument Moesha had with her father. Her independent streak had been growing, and now it seemed to be in control, especially when she slammed the door as she walked out of the house. The argument was so bad that everyone was left wondering if she'd even be back again. And, if she came back, how could she and Frank mend the fences they'd broken?

She'd be back, of course. It wouldn't be a new season without all the Mitchells together under one roof. But things might never be quite the same again. The new season would see Mo as a senior. What would happen to her? Where would she go to college? Would she still be determined to be a journalist? How would life change for her?

One way life looked as if it might alter was the possible introduction of a new interest. Because of his other commitments, Usher wouldn't be able to return as Jeremy. There had been discussions, however, about bringing rapper Mase into the show (handily, he was managed by Sonja Norwood). He might not be a boyfriend, but just someone "interested in Moesha," according to sources.

And his might not be the only new face on *Moesha*. There had been discussions about bringing Mekhi Phifer, who would appear with Brandy in the video for "The Boy Is Mine" and also in *I Still Know What You Did*

Last Summer, into the show as a teacher at Bridgewood.

The show had changed and evolved, but that was exactly what it needed to do. The characters had to grow, even if it wasn't always in a perfect way. That growth allowed the show to confront a lot of different issues that hit home with teens, and to be realistic. Relationships change as time passes, and *Moesha* reflected that. People find themselves in different situations, with different people. The nature of friendships alters, and the show was trying to illustrate all that. There'd been less of the cutesy, trivial episodes, and more that explored deeper emotional issues, without every forgetting that it was, after all, still a sitcom. No preaching, no melodrama, just a light, deft touch in the acting and the writing.

By now there could be no doubt that Brandy had established herself as an actress, a television star. But just in case anyone had forgotten in the couple of years since her last big single, she was still very much a singer, too. And she was about to prove it.

ELEVEN

The finishing touches had been put on Brandy's new record while *Moesha* took a short break over Christmas 1997. It had taken a long time to reach this stage, but finally, it was complete, and out of her hands.

For someone who'd been so nervous about even making a second album, once she began work she'd become very involved in every stage of it. But that was fine. Now it really mattered to her.

It still had to find the ideal slot on the schedule, and sometime in the summer seemed like the perfect bet. For a start, she'd be free then to publicize it. For the early part of the year, her schedule was full, first with *Moesha*, and then with her debut featured movie role. After the success of *Brandy*, and her much higher profile, this album, to be titled *Never Say Never*, was really going to be pushed hard.

Perhaps the biggest surprise was that it wouldn't be entirely a solo effort. Of the sixteen tracks, two would be duets, both with people whose names were quickly becoming recognizable—Mase and Monica.

Brandy had met Mase not long after she turned eighteen, while she was still dating Wayna Morris. It was at a party in New York for LL Cool J. He asked her to dance, and that was exactly what they did.

"He was so cute," she recalled. "But I didn't think anything would come of it."

Certainly she'd never expected anything in the way of business and music. But a few months later, Sonja Norwood happened to run into one of Mase's representatives, and the two started talking. With all she'd done for Brandy and Ray J., it was obvious she was good at making things happen, and so a decision was made to have her bring Mase into her management stable.

"Naturally, I was thrilled," Brandy said.

The two of them began hanging out together. The West Coast was her home, but he was a New Yorker, who introduced her to a lot of the city that she didn't know.

"He's taken me out a couple of times. He's shown me Harlem. We hang out a lot, but as far as a relationship goes, nope. But he's the sweetest guy. One time this bum came up to the car and said, 'Can you help me out?' Mase gave him a hundred dollars. I was so impressed."

Inevitably, the tabloids began pairing them up, once they were seen together, particularly after a party thrown by Sean "Puffy" Combs, which ended in a brawl, Mase in the thick of the action, and Brandy comforting him afterwards. She'd been there, and she comforted him. But that was the end of the story.

"He's not my type," she admitted. "I like those guys that . . . hmm. I don't know. Mase is my friend . . . I don't have a boyfriend. I'm *so* single right now. It's better that way. Guys are . . . Mase probably has millions of women."

He was certainly successful enough. His album, *Harlem World,* had been almost as massive as Brandy's debut, selling more than three million copies. The summer of '98 saw him all over the *Billboard* singles chart, helping out Cam'Ron on "Horse and Carriage," and with his own "Lookin' At Me" featuring the ubiquitous Puff Daddy.

Having him work with Brandy on "Top of the World" just seemed perfectly natural.

"We thought it would be a good idea," Brandy said. "It would give people something to talk about. Plus, I am a big fan of Mase's music."

It was a winning combination, even though their images were complete opposites. Brandy was still very much the good girl, the girl next door, while Mase was the man of the world, the bad boy, so cool he was almost made of ice, street-wise and dangerous.

Quite where it would all lead remained to be seen. Although Brandy denied any kind of a relationship between the two of them, they were together, arm in arm, and the MTV Movie Awards, both dressed in white. Then they met up again at a party. Brandy arrived with her mom, but Mase soon joined them (he had said that "she and her mom are family. I spend a lot of time with them whenever they're in New York or when I go to California"), and witnesses reported the pair, holding hands and embracing, with them finally leaving together, shielded by Sonja and some security guards.

It was the other duet that would attract more immediate attention, however. On "The Boy is Mine,"

Brandy teamed up with another teen R&B singer, Monica, for what would prove to be *the* summer hit of 1998. Released as a single in May, before *Never Say Never*, it soared to the top of the charts, staying there for weeks on end, a total of two months, before falling, only to go back to Number One at the end of August. It was a track America just couldn't get enough of. The video, directed by Joseph Khan, and featuring Mekhi Phifer as the two-timing man busted by two ladies, seemed to be in permanent rotation on MTV. The track was also on *Never Say Never* and also gave the title to Monica's newest album.

At seventeen, Monica was a couple of years younger than Brandy. But, like her, she'd first hit the big-time early, with *Miss Thang* in 1995. Back then, a lot of people had wondered about her, particularly with the single "Don't Take It Personal (Just One of Dem Days)," which seemed way too mature for a fourteen-year-old girl.

"I didn't want to do the bubblegum thing," Monica said. "There were enough people doing it."

Instead, she came across with a decided attitude. She was tough, and she seemed as if she had a big chip on her shoulder, although that was really more on record than in real life.

Like Brandy, though, Monica was very mature for her age. She was tutored while she was on tour, and managed to graduate a year early from Atlanta Country Day School with a 4.0 GPA—hardly a dummy.

She'd grown up in College Park, Georgia, with her mother Marilyn, and her stepfather, the Reverend Dr.

E.J. Best, Jr., although she did reconcile with her biological father not too long ago.

Monica's career really began in 1992, when a talent scout introduced her to Dallas Austin, a record producer who became her mentor. Like Brandy, though, Monica had begun by singing in church, also starting when she was two.

"She was always singing," her mother recalled. "She would have a pencil or a flashlight—anything—using it as a pretend microphone, and just sing her little heart out."

Austin would be one of the producers on "The Boy Is Mine." For some reason, people in the media had decided that Brandy and Monica should be enemies, even though that had never been the case. They knew each other, and respected each other, and there'd never been any bad words between them—in fact, there'd never been much close contact at all.

A phone call brought them closer.

"[W]e got to be friends before we worked together," Brandy recalled. "On the phone, we talked about clothes, guys, or what songs we like or what we're working on . . . and once I started to get to know her, I realized we had similar interests."

What better way was there for them to prove everyone wrong than to pair up on a song?

"Monica's talented, and I'm doing my thing. So why do we have to be enemies?" Brandy wondered. And indeed they didn't. Indeed, after Brandy had finished co-writing the song, she was the one who picked Monica for the duet.

"That girl has an amazing enthusiasm for her work,"

Monica said of Brandy. "She has a fun way of taking situations that are dark and lightening them up."

Once the record was out, the public perception of the pair definitely changed.

"People come up to me asking, 'Where's Monica?' because they know we're friends. She's a very real, down-to-earth person."

It was almost as if they were *destined* to be friends. In spite of the two-year age gap between them, they had too much in common not be become close buds. Both of them had started their recording careers young, and known instant success with their first albums, before they'd really had a chance to find themselves. And academically, both were high achievers. They pushed themselves as hard as they could. Monica might not have had any acting aspirations, but if she had, it would have been a sure bet that she'd have made it.

Under all the glitz and glamor that came with stardom, they were both normal teenagers, both finding it hard to get real boyfriends, which made the song particularly apt. Neither knew whether a boy they'd meet liked them for themselves, or because of their status—that was true of any new friend, in fact.

Each of them still had academic aspirations. Brandy was still enrolled at Pepperdine in Malibu, even though she was unable to take a heavy course load. Monica, too was planning for college, and, like Brandy, wanted to major in psychology, which made Brandy something of a mentor and role model for her, as well as a friend.

"I have to be focused," Monica said. "I can't do college the way I did high school. Monica is going on *Monica's* money, and I want to get all that I can out of the experience. I want to get everything I can out of life."

Her own single and album followed "The Boy Is Mine" very handily up the charts, ensuring Monica much more success on her own terms.

Before "The Boy is Mine" appeared, Brandy was full of nerves about it.

"Do you think people will like it?" she asked a friend. "Do you think they'll buy it?"

Soon there was no doubt about what they'd do. It served as both a taster and a teaser for the new album, which had rapidly become eagerly anticipated as the song was played more and more. But there was a gap of more than two months between the single and the appearance of the whole album.

It was going to be a bit of a surprise to those who were expecting more of *Brandy*. This was someone who'd grown up a lot in the intervening four years, and wanted everyone to realize it. The black-and-white cover shot announced the intention immediately. Deliberately glamorous, it showed half of Brandy's face, accenting her lips, her big, oval eye, and her flawless skin, framed by those famous braids. She looked like a model (which, indeed, she was now). The picture on the back, of her sitting in a chair, made her look more her age, a big grin on her face, but there were no doubts that the kid had been left far behind. Brandy was now an adult.

Perhpas the biggest shock was that David Foster, who'd been responsible for a number of middle-of-the-road ballads, was the producer of a couple of tracks, one, "Have You Ever?" by songstress Diane Warren, who'd been creating chart hits for years for any number of artists, including Celine Dion, and the other a cover of "(Everything I Do) I Do It For You," the song from *Robin Hood: Prince of Thieves*, the 1991 Kevin Costner film, which had been such a massive worldwide hit for Canada's Bryan Adams. They seemed a move away from her R&B image. But then again, with Cinderella, Brandy had established herself as much more of an *entertainer*, able to put songs across that had absolutely nothing to do with R&B. It was her album, and there was absolutely no reason why she couldn't include exactly what she wanted.

It all began with a lulling intro, and Brandy singing the title of the album like a mantra before going into "Angel in Disguise," a song to a male friend who'd fallen for the wrong girl—someone he thought was the right girl—and had his heart broken, never realizing that it was Brandy who loved him the whole time. Musically it set the tone for the whole record. Brandy's voice had come a long, long way in four years. She'd obviously spent a lot of time working with her vocal coach (her dad), and the results were immediately evident. Apart from sounding more adult, there was a lot more control, and a wider range than she'd shown on *Brandy*. On a mid-paced tune like this, she could still wind herself around the lines, and project emotion into the lyrics. It was R&B as pop music, the new pop music, all over the charts, all based around an urgent, killer rhythm that just couldn't be ignored.

But nowhere near as poppy as *the* song, "The Boy Is Mine." Brandy and Monica worked perfectly on this story of rivalry, which really made fun of the dislike they were supposed to have for each other, in as good a song as would be released in 1998, and one which could only have been catchier if it had been covered in hooks. They traded off verses and provided the vocal backings while the tune fizzed lightly behind them. Brandy had co-written this one, working on the lyrics, and it was apparent that she'd become a very assured composer as well as singer. Everything meshed so perfectly that you couldn't imagine this being anything but a hit as the girls gently dissed each other. Some called it the "estrogen flip" of the Paul McCartney/Michael Jackson hit, "The Girl Is Mine," but this was much, much better, never insipid or weak. Brandy and Monica injected real personality and fun into this, even if the guy never did get his just desserts in the song for two-timing them.

The first of the slow jams, "Learn the Hard Way," followed, and it needed a change of pace to work. Again, Brandy had worked on the lyrics, about a man who'd hurt her so badly she couldn't love him any more. The tune was appealing, and the intricate vocal work, again all by Brandy, made it sound lush and full, and actually not a million miles from some of the songs one of her inspirations, Stevie Wonder, had written. Was it about Wayna Morris? Probably not directly, but it was very likely inspired by the heartache she'd felt after they broke up. The young teen love aspect of *Brandy* was gone now; the issues, while still innocent—Brandy would never get sleazy, anyway—had moved on from the simplicity of high school boyfriend and girlfriend, into the more complex attitudes of the adult world. The emotions might not change, but somehow the settings had.

It all dissolved with some lovely guitar work, and segued straight into "Almost Doesn't Count." It was a song about a guy who couldn't quite commit, who was close to falling in love with her, but never quite able to make the final push. It continued the slightly melancholy mood that seemed to cover most of the album. The song had an almost jazzy vibe, with sophisticated keyboards behind the vocals. It was classy, and swung on a soft groove, very deep in the pocket. Brandy sounded more womanly here than on any of the previous tracks, handling the romantic situation with resignation, knowing it wasn't going to work out with a man like that.

One of the big surprises about "Top of the World" was that it hadn't been written by Brandy, since it seemed to deal so specifically with her situation. Yes, she was famous now, and rich. But that didn't make her any different from the person she'd always been, even if she seemed to be spending her time on top of the world these days. What people imagined her to be like and reality were two different things. She still hung with her homies, still did the things she'd always done. And money didn't buy the answers to all the big questions. The rap from Mase that opened the song and punctuated it in the middle was as low-key as Brandy's vocal. Like her, this was a man who had confidence in himself, who knew that what people saw was distorted from the real man, while the groove moved thickly behind them.

It was worth noting that *Never Say Never* seemed to generally have more of a unified sound than its predecessor, thanks in large part to the producers. Most of the tracks found Rodney Jerkins behind the controls (although his brother, Fred, had handled "Almost Doesn't Count," his own composition), and he kicked up the percussion, particularly the bell that gave "Angel in Disguise" its distinctive feel. It was only the mainstream tunes that brought in other producers, the bigger ballads.

R&B had changed in the four years since *Brandy*. Things could be more low-key now, and that really worked in favor of Brandy's low register, which intertwined with the instruments and went slinking around the mix. She wasn't, and would never be, an out-and-out diva like Whitney. She did her own thing, and did it very well. This was a different generation, and it was in command now. The divas would still have their audience, but this was what was fly. This was about the rhythm, and when you had a good one—and *Never Say Never* was full of them, thanks to Rodney Jerkins—you just rode it. There were debts to Timbaland, who resurrected the groove in R&B, and also Jam and Lewis, who'd helped keep it alive for years, particularly in their work with Janet Jackson. But this record had a sound that was very much its own, instantly identifiable. It was still very definitely Brandy on top, her album, but she had the tunes to carry it all.

Even on first hearing, with less than half the tracks done, it was obvious that this had megahit written all over it. Brandy had stepped up to the plate for a second time, and once again hit the ball right out of the park. That much was obvious when the album entered the chart at Number Ten, and a week later had already sold over a million copies—impressive by anyone's standards, even if the pump had been primed by the major success of "The Boy is Mine."

"U Don't Know Me (Like U Used To)" had that

Jerkins groove again, another song about a faithless lover, the main underlying theme of this record, it seemed. Nothing on the disc would be faster than midpace, but it didn't need to be. Any quicker and it wouldn't have suited Brandy's voice at all, or any of the emotions that were being expressed. And the whole cool sense of it would have vanished. While Brandy's voice worked best on the slow jams, she could easily pick up on this type of song, too, and handle it perfectly, coaxing a feel out of a word or a line. The girl and her producers knew exactly what they were doing.

"Never Say Never," the album's title track, was something a little different—a real love song. But even in that, there were people trying to pull the couple apart, to tear them away from each other, who thought they'd never get together in the first place. Co-written again by Brandy, it was touching, with a great vocal arrangement that built up Brandy's voice, layer by layer, trading off backgrounds and leads in the way that had almost become her trademark now, something a lot of other artists had copied along the way. The Brandy of this track was determined (just like the girl herself). Nothing was going to tear this couple apart, no matter what other people thought.

Now it was time for a change of pace. After seven tracks of Brandy's personal take on R&B, she decided to throw in a couple of ballads, big ballads. Not quite Celine Dion, not even Whitney, but big enough by her own standards. "Truthfully" was produced by Marc Nelson, one of the song's composers, and it stood in real contrast to all the songs that had gone before. There weren't the grand gestures and long, sustained notes other singers might have put in. That wasn't the style of this girl. She could sell a song without any of that. It came as a big of a shock, a jerk, after everything that had gone before, and abruptly altered the mood. While it showed that Brandy could handle all this, the problem was that "Truthfully" wasn't a great song. There was no hook, either in the lyrics or the music, that reached out and grabbed the listener, and the production, full as it was, still seemed somehow empty, missing some textures to set it apart from a thousand other ballads.

Just how much it was missing became evident by setting it next to "Have You Ever?", Diane Warren's song, which was produced by David Foster. Warren had penned any number of hits, and she and Foster had worked together before—they'd been responsible for at least two Number One hits, Celine Dion's "Because You Loved Me" and Toni Braxton's "Un-break My Heart." They were the epitome of professionalism, giving a full, rich sound to the track, and enough of a story in the song—not to mention a powerful chorus—to keep the listener involved. Given the fact that Brandy obviously wanted to widen the range of her song material, it wasn't too strange that she'd go to these two, where you knew exactly what you'd get, and that it would sound good. Still, however, she came nowhere near diva territory.

A kick back into an R&B groove followed, with Rodney Jerkins putting it on thick and heavy with "Put That On Everything," where Brandy (who co-wrote) offered to do anything and everything for the guy she loved. Mid-paced, it was a great way to return from the ballads. This was the real deal, a reminder that Brandy might be showing more facets on *Never Say Never*, but she wasn't abandoning the music she loved.

"In the Car Interlude" was exactly that, even if it probably wasn't really taped in Brandy's wheels. But the idea of her starting the vehicle, some funky beat playing in the background, and of her talking to her producers on the car phone gave the little piece a very hip-hop, street feel, just another reminder that she wasn't going to be totally forsaking her roots anytime soon.

The magic continued with "Happy," where once again Rodney Jerkins conjured up the spell of the endless groove, and Brandy helped pen the words, that, as the title implied, were a straight-up love song, wound around some low-key funk. There was passion behind the voice, and you had to wonder if Brandy wasn't singing about some real person in her life (could it be Mase?) that she was hiding from everybody. Whoever it was about—and the same applied to "Put That On Everything"—was a lucky guy.

Never Say Never was almost a State of Brandy speech, a way of saying that here was where she stood, these were the things she could do, accept me for who I am, not what you think I might be. The reality of her shone through every track, and with over sixty-six minutes of music, there was a lot of Brandy to hear, an opportunity for her to show many different sides of herself. Her voice, and her power, had grown by leaps and bounds over the last four years. It was stronger, and while she still rode the grooves, she never got lost in them, always staying slightly above them in control of the situation, making the music work for *her*.

Exactly what she could do with the music was shown

on "One Voice." This, too, had David Foster at the controls, and the music was something that *really* took Brandy back to her roots, all the way to the gospel music she first head, and first sang, in church when she was a little kid. And it brought out a side of her that hadn't been heard before. Anyone who thought that Brandy couldn't wail in real gospel fashion was in for a very big surprise. She had it in her to take the roof off a church if she really wanted, and that was exactly what she did on a few occasions during the song. Most of the album had been very restrained, but this just let loose. It was exactly what she needed to do, even if it stood in very sharp contrast of everything else on the disc. If she ever contemplated an record of gospel songs, she'd be able to carry it off with no problem; it was in her blood, that much was obvious.

"Tomorrow," the sixth song on the record that Brandy had co-written (a sure sign of her hands-on involvement with this album) cooled it all down with a very righteous slow jam. It was a song about preparing to leave someone who'd treated her badly, and the idea that tomorrow, when she made the change, things would begin to seem brighter. Like everything Rodney Jerkins produced, there was a groove, this time slow and thick, not unlike some of Toni Braxton's material. It was a good song to really start the wind-down, swaying along, just chillin' as the night fell.

If the album contained a single big kick, among many, it was the final track, her re-make of the Bryan Adams hit "(Everything I Do) I Do It For You." Back in 1991 it had been a huge international hit for Adams, spending seven weeks at Number One. It had been a soppy ballad then, with Adams's gravelly voice trying to catch and hold the notes. It seemed the unlikeliest thing for Brandy. But when it arrived, it was hard to find the original any more. David Foster had given the entire song a makeover, and now it sounded brand-new and custom-tailored for Brandy. Where Adams had gone out of his way to inject the histrionics, Brandy kept it all low-key and intimate, propelled along by a tidy little piano line, and a very soft groove. It *worked*. Unlike the first version, this sounded cool, not dumb, and what had seemed like fake passion seven years before now came across as very much the real thing, a spoken conversation with a very close boyfriend.

And that was it. *Never Say Never* was over. Sixteen tracks that let everyone know that Brandy was moving up from being the princess to the queen. This was a girl who had it all going on, and wasn't afraid to show it. The things that had attracted people to her voice in the first place were still there, but she'd added to them, taken on entire new dimensions. There was no doubt it was a total winner.

TWELVE

But it wasn't just the album that was a winner. Everything Brandy touched seemed to turn to gold—if not platinum. Before *Never Say Never* even appeared in the stores, she was taking her career to an entirely new level by making her first featured performance in a movie. And not just any movie, but *I Still Know What You Did Last Summer*, the sequel to the phenomenally sucessful horror flick *I Know What You Did Last Summer*.

I Know had been written by Kevin Williamson, the man who'd authored the incredible hit *Scream*, as well as being the creative brains behind the series *Dawson's Creek*. He had his finger on the pulse, he knew what people wanted to see. *I Know* had been made on what was little more than a shoestring budget, but on its release in November 1997, it had done some very serious box office business, bringing in over $71 million. That was more than enough impetus to quickly come up with a sequel. While it wouldn't be written by Williamson, who had a ton of projects on his plate, he'd actually written the treatment for the film when he penned the original.

The first film had had two very cool teen stars, Jennifer Love Hewitt *(Party of Five, Can't Hardly Wait)* and Sarah Michelle Gellar *(Buffy the Vampire Slayer)*. Gellar's character had met a sticky end at the end of the mysterious fisherman's hook. Hewitt's character, Julie James, had survived, along with her boyfriend, Ray (Freddie Prinze, Jr.). She'd gone back to college, and was doing well, although the end of the movie came with a scary cliffhanger, the words "I Still Know" written in the steam of a shower glass, and then the glass shattering.

This time around, the movie would have a much more exotic setting than a fishing community in the Carolinas. Julie James and her college friend would be fighting off the man in the sou'wester and waders in Bermuda.

Brandy would play the friend, a girl working her way through college as a waitress, whose hobby, conveniently enough, happened to be kickboxing. She'd be the one who won the trip, not quite realizing that a vacation in paradise wasn't going to be all she expected.

As producer Neil Moritz commented, "With a sequel, you've got to top the first one. You've got to make it scarier. So that's what we're trying to do—scare the hell out of people."

I Know had not only been scary, but Williamson's words had also been funny. Could first-time writer Trey Callaway do the same? In November 1998 people would be able to find out for themselves.

The movie might have been largely set in Bermuda,

but none of the filming took place there. Instead, Mexico offered a sunnier and cheaper substitute. The production set up in Manzanillo, a resort town. For Brandy, it was quite literally the first time she'd really been away from her family. At first she'd wanted Sonja to come along with her for the several weeks of the location shooting, but Sonja, busy taking care of the careers of Mase and Ray J., was simply too busy. Once she arrived, Brandy was glad she'd come alone.

"[W]hen I got here, I thought, 'I'm cool. I'm chillin'.' So I'm kinda glad she's busy. She doesn't have to worry about me. I'm a grown-up person."

But even though she was grown-up, that didn't mean she wanted to be totally isolated in Mexico. Her phone bill during the shoot totalled a pretty impressive $8,000, as she spent a lot of her free time on the phone with her family and friends.

Onscreen, however, was definitely a new Brandy. The innocent of *Moesha* and *Cinderella* were light-years behind. In the movie, Julie James would be making the trip with her boyfriend, Ray. And Brandy's character would be bringing *her* boyfriend, played by Mekhi Phifer, who seemed to be spending all his screen time around Brandy in 1998 (he was even being considered for a role on *Moesha*). As part of the plot, the couple would be enjoying some serious make-out time. Mo might have swapped a kiss with Q, but it was nothing like this.

There'd be another first, too, as audiences got to see Brandy's navel for the first time. It might not seem like that big of a deal, but on the previous season of *Moesha*,

Sonja Norwood had vetoed a suggestion to have Brandy's belly button showing.

This Brandy would be a young woman of real substance and sass, definitely not always playing by the rules, and kicking some very serious fisherman butt along the way. Anyone going to watch the movie thinking Brandy would be the meek and mild girl they thought they knew was going to be in for a very major surprise, and come away with a completely revised opinion, which was exactly what Brandy wanted.

She'd been stereotyped, but the perception of her was a long way from reality. Yes, at heart she was still very sweet, but she was no longer fifteen years old. Time had passed, and she'd grown and changed. She wasn't any one thing, but like everyone else, had a number of different sides, and wanted everyone to realize that there was a lot more to her than they thought.

Brandy had been in films before, but never as a featured player. The work schedule was long and tough. And it was also quite hazardous at times. Some of the filming was done in a mango grove, and the cast occasionally found themselves being hit by scorpions falling out of the trees, as well as a species of beetle with very acidic pee.

"People were always whacking each other to get the bugs off. It was pretty gross," recalled Jennifer Love Hewitt.

When everything was wrapped, it was back to the peace and bug-free environment of the San Fernando Valley for Brandy, and to the house she shared with her parents and her brother, as well as her two dogs.

It was also a return to the insecurity that seemed to haunt her, and kept driving her.

"Do people like my show because of Countess?" she wondered. "Did people watch *Cinderella* because of Whitney?" And now she had a new one to add to the list. "*I Still Know What You Did Last Summer* is going to be a hit, but will it be because of Jennifer?"

While it was true that a lot of people would be going to the movie because of Love, who'd become a sizable star in her own right, Brandy didn't need to worry too much. There'd be a big crowd there because of her, particularly after *Never Say Never* had done so well immediately upon its release, and with her having spent most of the summer at Number One. Together, Brandy and Jennifer Love Hewitt should make an unstoppable team. They might not be carrying home any Oscars for their work, but, for now at least, that was just fine. They'd be packing them in at the multiplexes; the film was going to be huge even before its release. The acting awards could wait for later in their careers. The Academy had a problem with horror films, anyway.

It had been an interesting experience for Brandy, but the last twelve months had been full of interesting experiences, from *Cinderella* to the feistier version of Moesha, from her new album and hot, hot single to this film. It would have been impossible to have packed any more into the span of a single year. Had she given Hewitt (who had CDs of her own out, in a definite R&B vein, on the same label as Brandy) any singing tips? If she had, no one was saying. Had Hewitt helped her with her acting? They were equals, people who'd both worked long and hard, over many years, to get where they were now. Above all, they were both professionals, both wanting to challenge themselves and conquer all types of fields. Hewitt had moved into movie production and writing, with *Cupid's Arrow*, due for release in 1999. Brandy was eager to do some record production, to direct a TV show or a movie. They were the people who'd still be making waves in ten and twenty years, the ones with ambition.

For Brandy, success meant the chance to do anything and everything. There were more acting opportunities being offered every day, and one that she was seriously considering was a project with Oprah Winfrey, whose adaptation of Toni Morrison's novel, *Beloved*, would be appearing in theaters a month before Brandy's own film.

The future could hardly have been brighter. Everything had gone her way. And now there was a fourth season of *Moesha* ahead of her, with Mo now a senior, on the cusp of some major changes. And that raised questions about where the show might go, and if it might continue past this season, taking her to college—certainly, the possibilities were endless.

Like her fictional counterpart, Brandy Norwood had said at one time that she'd like to be a journalist one day. That seemed a little more up in the air, however. In her own college career, her major had gone from psychology to English, before passing to "undecided."

"I have to think about taking more college courses at Pepperdine in September, doing the show, and the release of my new album. I've never done so much before—but with some good discipline and a good family and crew behind me, I can definitely do it."

It had been three years since Brandy had been out on tour. In that time, she'd only appeared once as a singer, as a guest on brother Ray J.'s Disney Channel special. But having *Never Say Never* out there, and doing so well (as well as America, it had charted in Britain, where "The Boy Is Mine" was also a major hit) meant a responsibility to her fans, and Brandy was planning a series of dates for spring of 1999.

Why so far ahead? Well, with her schedule, that would be the first free time she'd have, after taping the new season of *Moesha*. Where she'd play, how long the tour would be, and all the other details still had to be worked out. But there was no doubt in anyone's mind that every date would be sold right out.

When *that* was complete, she'd be able to spend time working on another movie over the summer. There'd be no rest for her, but she wasn't ready for any yet. This was a girl who could get mobbed in the streets in New York after she performed with Mase at the MTV Movie Awards, in one of the most cynical cities in the world. Everyone wanted her.

Some were willing to pay a lot to have her. In the summer of 1998 she became a spokeperson for Cover Girl makeup, as well as Candie's shoes, along with other artists as different as Lil' Kim and Shania Twain. Brandy would be part of the footwear company's fall campaign, her face (and her feet) plastered everywhere. It might not have been back on the catwalk at Milan, but it was still modeling.

Life has changed a lot since little Brandy Norwood

took a deep breath and began work on *Thea*. In five years her entire world has turned upside down, almost beyond recognition. But that was what she wanted, that was what she aimed for. These days, as she sang, she's quite literally on top of the world, living in a place where everyone seems to know her name and her face. And it couldn't have happened to a nicer person.

THIRTEEN

❖

For Brandy, growing up in the spotlight has meant it's been hard to enjoy a real life. People assume that the characters she's played have been her. While it's true she's far from wild, she's not totally Ms. Goody Two Shoes, either. To those outside, the image has wrongly become the person. They believe that " 'Brandy would never do this. Brandy would never say that.' " And that's not neceassrily the case, Brandy said: "Because the things people say Brandy wouldn't do, Brandy's done. And the things people say Brandy wouldn't say, Brandy's said."

By her own admission, she's no angel. The girl who was voted one of *People* magazine's Fifty Most Beautiful people is beautiful—that's simply beyond question, with those oval eyes, perfect skin, and long, long braids. But she's more than a picture, or what anyone sees on TV or hears on a stereo. She has her own life to live, and she has to live it, even if the reality clashes with the way people imagine her to be.

"The Brandy image is, I'm a kind, gentle virgin," she explained. "I'm nineteen! If I want to have sex, I have every right to. If I don't want to have sex, that's my business, too... You have two groups of people: those who think Brandy's a virgin, and those who think Brandy's lying. Well, I can't please everybody. I'm a real person, and I have a left side in me, too."

The true reality is that she's as full of contradictions and questions as anyone else. In her case, being in the public eye means that every little thing is noticed and blown out of all proportion. Who she's seen with, even what she eats. Like so many teenagers, Brandy can't cook—when would she have the time, anyway? So she eats her favorite food quite often—McDonald's cheeseburgers and french fries.

She is who she is, and you'd better accept it. Yes, she's a role model, and you'd never find her advocating anything bad. You'd never *find* her doing anything bad; that's simply not in her. Her parents have instilled a moral compass that points her very surely in the right direction. Church remains the constant it's always been in her life, and her faith is an important guiding factor for her. When she eventually does settle down and marry, "I want to raise my kids in God."

That, however, remains a long way off.

For now, she's still in a tricky place. People have expectations of her, and she can't upset those too much. It's a very fine line, as she understands.

"Sometimes I feel bad about people thinking I'm a goody-goody. I don't want my fans to see me smoking weed or falling over drunk in a club. People think this is a fairy-tale life, but they are so wrong. They may think that they want to be where I am, which is flattering, but they don't know what I go through. It's a lot of work to sell records and be on TV at the same time."

She acknowledges her responsibilities to her fans, but she needs a certain amount of freedom as she goes about discovering who she is, and about life in general.

"I can't get a bad reputation or my career will be over," she complained. "And that's what I don't like. I don't want to have a perfect image. I want room to make mistakes."

Which, of course, is precisely what everyone needs, at any time.

Brandy's become a teen role model now. It's not so much by choice; she's simply one of the most visible teenagers around. That means her look, her attitude, and even her clothes are copied by lots of girls. She might buy Polo, Tommy Hillfiger, DKNY and the other designers, but it's the way she puts them all together that sets the trends.

"I never started out saying, 'I am Ms. Fashion Plate,' " she said. "All I have ever done is have a fun time wearing what I wear and maybe venturing out onto a limb where other people won't. I've had outfits with thigh-high stockings and white "space boots," and yet it looked wholesome, not really freaky."

The girl has taste and good fashion sense. But she just knows how to look good, period. She doesn't like to use much makeup, in part because she really doesn't need it. Her skin is remarkably clear, her dark eyes shine very brightly. Because she spends so much of her time in the public eye, she does have her own makeup artist, Nzingha, who sometimes travels with her. She's part of the crew, along with Sonja, Chrissy Murray, Brandy's publicist, and Brandy's personal assistant, her cousin Portia.

And, of course, she has a stylist, Kimberly Kimble, who takes care of those amazing braids—with the help of two other assistants, weaving either human or synthetic braids in there, along with Brandy's own hair.

"Having braids reduces the number of 'bad hair days,'" Brandy said, explaining why she'd kept the style. "To care for them at home, I just wash, condition, and oil them regularly using Aveda shampoos and conditioners."

Kimble redoes the braids regularly, an operation that takes eight hours.

"I like my braids best when they are fresh and lying straight down my back. People say I look like Pocahontas when I wear them like this."

And that's her preferred way of wearing them, although she's been known to gather them back casually, and "before I go to bed at night, I tie my braids up in a hair wrap so they stay straight and neat." To keep those braids straight between visits from Kimble, "I put oil on the hair and dip them in hot water."

On *Moesha*, Brandy's tried a lot of different, funky 'dos. But for herself, the braids are definitely it.

She's beautiful; *People* was certainly right about that. But beauty, the saying goes, is only skin-deep, and that's something Brandy recognizes all too well. People may go on about her looks, the slope of her cheekbones, the shape of her eyes, her skin, but that's not what's really important.

"Beauty comes from within. It's personality, it's morals. Beauty can be a lot of internal qualities. It's not just appearances."

But first impressions still count to a lot of people, and Brandy makes a very strong impression wherever she goes. Unless, of course, she's just relaxing and chillin' with her homies—something she doesn't get too much time to do any more. There's her long-time best friend, Joi, Tracey (Brandy's godsister), Portia, the cousin who works with her, and Chaz, her male bud.

"I carve out time just to be by myself, and I invite friends over to my house for lunch and just hang out. Sometimes we go to the mall, because I like shopping."

To say Brandy likes shopping would be something of an understatement. Being so recognizable makes going to the mall a lot harder than it used to be, but it's something she still manages to find time for, to hit all the clothes stores and just fill her SUV with bags. But she's always loved to shop.

"When I first started making a little money, I went to BCBG, like, *every* week! Bought skirts, shoes—you know, those simple little business-type suits and stuff for my appearances. And I had a *good* time!"

Her friends, along with her family, are the people she can trust. Around them, she doesn't have to be on her guard. She can be the real Brandy, away from the image, away from all the pressures.

Pressure is something she's had to get used to, and it just continues, relentlessly. Every minute of every day is accounted for, from the moment she wakes until she falls into bed at night. It's one of the trade-offs of fame, and it's one she's coped with very well. It's a lot of work, as she admits, but the rewards are great. Not just in terms of money, but in the satisfaction of making people happy, and leaving herself fulfilled.

This was what she was born to do, to entertain, and she's still in the process of discovering just how far she can go. At nineteen, this is still the very tip of the iceberg. Two multi-platinum albums, a hit series, and a movie that's certain to be a box-office sensation would seem like a lot of peaks for most people, but really, Brandy's just beginning. She's a part of the new wave of teens to become big stars, virtually the same age as her fans, a figure they can easily relate to and understand. They can see themselves reflected in her.

From Leonardo DiCaprio to Jennifer Love Hewitt, from Hanson to Brandy, there's been a completely new pack of stars for a new generation, which is exactly as it should be. While a lot of women may find themselves still drooling over Brad Pitt, it's Leo who makes younger hearts beat faster. Bands like Hanson have shown that you don't have to be in your mid-twenties and plagued with angst to make music. This generation has come of age, and raised its own idols, the people they admire. And without exception, they're young. They stand for different things from their predecessors. When the Spice Girls talk about Girl Power, they're just putting into words the feelings of every young woman who's out there and wants her rights. They're not going to be used. Women have a power today that they never had before. They may still look at the boys, and put the posters on their walls, but they're also out there doing it for themselves. Exactly like Brandy.

These days it's not a black thing, or a white thing, or a Latino thing. It's a generational thing. The barriers of color don't mean what they used to. Hip-hop and R&B is as much the music of the suburbs as of the city. Fashion crosses every line. When the bass booms, everyone listens. And that's good. America is finally putting it all together, and getting rid of all its divisions. In her own quiet way, Brandy is helping that. Not just in her charity work (which remains important to her, even in these busy days), but just by being herself.

The world is changing, and for the better. The new stars have a style and savvy that goes beyond anything people expect. For the most part, they're people who've worked long and hard in show business, even if it seems as if they've been overnight sensations. They're professionals. You won't find Brandy or Hanson throwing prima donna fits, breaking things, having temper tantrums. They've become stars through ambition, desire, work, and a lot of talent.

"I wouldn't change a thing in my life," Brandy admitted. "I went from A to Z in this business. Now I know the ropes. I've made a lot of mistakes, but that happens. I always have my mother and brother for the added support I need."

But having come this far, it's not the end of the road, by any means.

"I'm blessed to have one day at a time. If God blesses me to live ten more years, I see myself acting, singing, directing, producing. But, more importantly, I see myself helping others. I have *lots* of goals for the future. I'm a big dreamer!"

What sets Brandy apart from other teens with all those big goals is the fact that she makes them happen. She's already done a little record production, on her new album (in fact, she was a co-producer on "The Boy is Mine"). She has determination. If she wants it to happen, you can bet that it will.

Maybe the thing that means most to her at present is the success of her record, having been so scared to make it. In the end, what she gave the world was a collection of songs that mean something to her.

"I only make music that I care about. I can't listen to the people who say I'm too good to be true. I'm just going to be my self. . . . my vocals come from my heart and my diaphragm. They come from my heart because I have matured in the four years since my last album."

It was her biggest challenge, but she overcame her nerves to produce the goods and add a lot of flava to 1998. Now, with its success, she'll have to do it again. But that's down the road. She has a couple of years before she even needs to think about a third album, and a lot can change in that time. Who can say where she'll be then, if *Moesha* will still be on television, whether Brandy will have become a movie star (which is a very strong bet).

One of the few certainties is that she'll never abandon music. There might be long, empty gaps between albums, but they will keep coming. Music has been her center for too long for her to ever abandon it completely. It's how she began, and it's one of the ways she'll continue. It's in her blood. Willie Norwood, who, apart from being her father is also her vocal coach, will keep her busy practicing, strengthening her voice, making it into an even more supple instrument.

And in 1999 there'll be the tour, a chance for fans old and new to see Brandy up on stage again. This time, though, she won't have to share the spotlight with any other groups. She'll be the headliner, a huge name now.

It's been a long path to reach that, though. Early on the highlights were few and far between, but Brandy Norwood kept singing, kept doing everything she could. The moment of that first recording contract, of the first time she held her own CD, of watching it rise up the charts, going platinum . . . all of those have been magical moments. She's crammed more memories, more living, into nineteen years than most people manage in a whole lifetime.

From here she can go anywhere she chooses. She'd be welcome on any project. But she'll pick and choose carefully. And, along the way, it's a given that she'll complete her degree. She may be rich now, but she knows that money in the bank isn't the same as an education.

Wherever she chooses to go, she'll keep looking for those challenges, the things to stretch her, whether in acting, music, or wherever. It's her nature never to be happy with the same old same old. You go, girlfriend.

"I love to be real and I love to be adventurous. I feel that in general, nothing ventured, nothing gained. You have to stick your neck out and do a lot of things."

And you know that's what she'll do. Always.

BRANDY ON THE WEB

If you've got a 'puter and a modem, a little surfing will get you a lot of Brandy. The sites seem to be increasing on a daily basis, which ought to be no real surprise.

The Official Brandy Site
(http://www.foreverbrandy.com)

is pretty cool. Nice pictures, even if it can be a bit threadbare on information.

The Unofficial Brandy Site
(http://www.brandy-fan.com)

has lots of good stuff. A good place to check out, and updated on a regular basis.

Carson Citizen
(http://www.gjw.com/Fans/Brandy.htm)

puts Brandy in the context of her California hometown, and makes it clear she's one of the leading citizens. Nice job.

Celebsite
(http://www.celebsite.com/people/brandy/index.html)

is pretty streamlined, but still does the job well.

**Brandy's Place
(http://www.ctrl-c.lio.se/~dreamlover/brandy/brandy.html)**

Great fansite. Lots of great info and photos.

DISCOGRAPHY

Brandy
(Atlantic, 1994)

Movin' On / Baby / Best Friend / I Wanna Be Down / I Dedicate (Part I) / Brokenhearted / I'm Yours / Sunny Day / As Long As You're Here / Always On My Mind / I Dedicate (Part II) / Love Is On My Side / Give Me You / I Dedicate (Part III)

Never Say Never
(Atlantic, 1998)

Intro / Angel In Disguise / The Boy Is Mine (Duet with Monica) / Learn The Hard Way / Almost Doesn't Count / Top Of The World (Featuring Mase) / U Don't Know Me (Like U Used To) / Never Say Never / Truthfully / Have you Ever? / Put That On Everything / In The Car Interlude / Happy / One Voice / Tomorrow / (Everything I Do) I Do It For You

Also Featured On:

Batman Forever (Original Soundtrack Album)
(1995)

"Where Are You Now" (with Lenny Kravitz)

Waiting To Exhale (Original Soundtrack Album)
(1996)

"Sittin' Up In My Room"

Set It Off (Original Soundtrack Album)

"Missing You" (with Tamia, Gladys Knight, and Chaka Khan)

FILMOGRAPHY

Arachnophobia (1990)
Demolition Man (1993)
I Still Know What You Did Last Summer (1998)

TELEVISION

Thea (ABC, 1993-94)
Brandy Norwood . . . Danesha Turrell
Thea Vidale . . . Thea Turrell
Adam Jeffries . . . Jarvis Turrell II
Jason Weaver . . . Jerome Turrell
Brenden Jefferson . . . James Turrell
Yvette Wilson . . . Lynette
Kenny Ford, Jr. . . . Leonard Thurman

Moesha (UPN, 1995-)
Brandy Norwood . . . Moesha Mitchell
Sheryl Lee Ralph . . . Dee Mitchell
William Allen Young . . . Frank Mitchell
Countess Vaughn . . . Kim Parker
Marcus T. Paulk . . . Myles Mitchell
Lamont Bently . . . Hakeem Campbell
Yvette Wilson . . . Andell

Cinderella (ABC, 1997)
Brandy . . . Cinderella
Whoopi Goldberg . . . Queen
Whitney Houston . . . Fairy Godmother
Jason Alexander . . . Lionel
Bernadette Peters . . . Stepmother
Paolo Montalban . . . Prince

Meet Hollywood's Coolest Young Superstar!

MATT DAMON

By Kathleen Tracy

Matt Damon is more than just a handsome heartthrob—he's also a talented actor and screenwriter who took home both a Golden Globe Award and an Oscar for co-writing the movie *Good Will Hunting*. Find out how he made it in Hollywood, what he plans for the future, about his lifelong friendship with Ben Affleck, about his steamy relationships with some of his leading ladies, and much, much more! Includes eight pages of exciting photos.

MATT DAMON
Kathleen Tracy
0-312-96857-4 _____ $4.99 U.S. _____ $6.50 CAN.

Publishers Book and Audio Mailing Service
P.O. Box 070059, Staten Island, NY 10307
Please send me the book(s) I have checked above. I am enclosing $_____ (please add $1.50 for the first book, and .50 for each additional book to cover postage and handling. Send check or money order only—no CODs) or charge my VISA, MASTERCARD, DISCOVER or AMERICAN EXPRESS card.

Card Number_____
Expiration date_____Signature_____
Name_____
Address_____
City_____State/Zip_____

Please allow six weeks for delivery. Prices subject to change without notice. Payment in U.S. funds only. New York residents add applicable sales tax.

DAMON 10/98

GET THE SIZZLING INSIDE STORY ON THE WORLD'S HOTTEST BAND!

BACKSTREET BOYS

They've Got it Goin' On!

Anna Louise Golden

Find out all about AJ, Brian, Howie, Kevin, and Nick—step into their world, see what makes them tick, what kind of girls they like, how they make their way-cool music, and much, much more! Includes eight pages of cool color photos.

BACKSTREET BOYS
Anna Louise Golden
0-312-96853-1_____ $3.99 U.S. _____ $4.99 CAN.

Publishers Book and Audio Mailing Service
P.O. Box 070059, Staten Island, NY 10307
Please send me the book(s) I have checked above. I am enclosing $_____ (please add $1.50 for the first book, and $.50 for each additional book to cover postage and handling. Send check or money order only—no CODs) or charge my VISA, MASTERCARD, DISCOVER or AMERICAN EXPRESS card.

Card Number_____
Expiration date_____ Signature_____
Name_____
Address_____
City_____ State/Zip _____

Please allow six weeks for delivery. Prices subject to change without notice. Payment in U.S. funds only. New York residents add applicable sales tax.

BOYS 10/98